MW00439834

The Judge's Bride
Montana Brides of Solomon's Valley
Valley
Book 1

By

Patricia PacJac Carroll

The Judge's Bride: Montana Brides of Solomon's Valley Book 1 by Patricia PacJac Carroll

Copyright © April 2017

Published by Patricia PacJac Carroll @ PacJac Publishing

Book Cover: Charlene Raddon at SilverSageBookCovers.com

For more information, please contact

email …………….. patricia@pacjaccarroll.com

Web site………….. pacjaccarroll.com

FB

https://www.facebook.com/PatriciaPacJacCarrollAutho r?ref=hl

Twitter   https://twitter.com/PacJac

Amazon page: Books by Patricia PacJac Carroll

**Sign up for my Newsletter. Friday Night at the Bookshelf and find out when my new books are releasing, sales, and just plain fun:

Friday Night at the Bookshelf: Patricia PacJac Carroll Newsletter > http://eepurl.com/bpPmbP

The Judge's Bride:
Montana Brides of Solomon's Valley
(Book 1)

.

Chapter 1

October 1881
Montana

Fierce pounding yanked Judge Solomon Taggart from his dream. He threw off the blanket, swung his feet to the floor, and groaned as they met the cold wood. More hard raps rattled the front door below as well as his usually mild temperament. "I'm coming!"

Bad enough they'd taken him from his sweet Clara, at least the dream of her, but now he'd been thrust into the chill of morning earlier than planned. After throwing on pants and shirt, he stomped to the main entryway, grabbed the longhorn door handle, and flung it open to find the reason for his inconvenience.

4

Matt Stearns, the young foreman of his ranch, fidgeted before him. Mussed hair, boots on the wrong feet, and unbuttoned shirt proved he'd been jolted out of the sack, too.

The judge motioned for the man to enter. "What's the trouble?"

Matt pointed toward the valley. "It's them kids of the Murphys and Howards. They're fighting over a half-grown calf on our land, and one of 'em has a gun."

"Who's watching them?"

"Fisher and Yates. Told 'em not to shoot. They're just kids."

"Get my horse. Better saddle Big Sandy, I'm not in the mood to deal with the black." The judge went to the gun rack and retrieved his favorite Winchester. He didn't plan to shoot anyone, but it made a good bargaining tool to diffuse these differences. Reminded of the cold, he grabbed his sheepskin jacket from the coat rack.

The Murphys and the Howards. Those two families were nothing but trouble. They were nice enough if you met them alone, but together, it was like mixing fire and nitro.

With a sigh, he stepped into the predawn morning and watched his breath fog the air. Why did those fool kids pick such a cold day for their nonsense? The chill crept into his forty-year-old bones and made him wonder just why it was his job to come between the feuding families.

As a former judge in Tennessee and owner of the Rockin' C, the largest ranch in the valley, the folks looked to him for leadership. Not that he minded. Except when it came on one of these bone-chilling mornings.

Matt rode to him, leading the big palomino that had been with the judge since he'd carved out his ranch. Sturdy and reliable, Big Sandy was just the horse for an early morning ride. He took the reins and mounted. "How far do we have to go?"

"They're out near Fork Creek."

"Let's get there before we have a tragedy." The judge nudged the stallion into an easy lope and headed for trouble.

Half an hour later, they rode up a ridge littered with scrub oak and brush. Below, maybe thirty head of Rockin' C cattle grazed on the slopes leading to the creek. To one side, a heifer was singled out, tied to a tree, and bellowing her head off.

"Where are the kids?"

Yated pointed to the rise opposite them and then to the brush near the calf. "Boy's on the ridge. Girl is in the brush. She's got a gun."

The judge winced. "The girl has a gun?"

"Rifle. And she knows how to shoot. She's kept the boy away from the cow."

"That half-grown heifer one of ours?" Solomon had fought for his cattle. Killed to protect what was his. But not a kid.

"Don't know. Can't see a brand. Fisher is with the boy. Hope you can talk some sense into that girl."

The judge felt old as he reined his horse down the ravine. He'd fought Indians, rustlers, and squatters, but how do you reason with a girl? He'd never had much luck with his daughter, Shirley, much less his wife, Clara. Ah, he missed them.

Throwing a glance heavenward, he sighed. *You were supposed to stay with me, honey. I wasn't ready for you to leave. Better if that fever had attacked me.* He'd have fought heaven and hell to stay with his family.

Shoving away the memories, he squinted into the brush. "Girl! It's Judge Solomon Taggart. I'm here to settle this dispute. Hold your fire."

The bushes in front of him parted. "It's me. Cassidy Howard. I came for my cow. She broke loose, and I tracked her here. That crazy Murphy boy tried to take her from me."

"Hold your fire. That goes for your temper *and* your gun." The judge dismounted. He stepped over a fallen log, walked to the young cow, and ran a hand over her left hip. No brand. Meant it wasn't one of his. Or if it was, it got past his crew, and that was unlikely.

"Cassidy, can you prove it's yours?" He studied the girl. With her wild blond hair and sky-blue eyes, she was going to be a beauty in a few years. Already, her womanhood was beginning to show, but it was going to take a tough young man to tame her. She had a temper to match the wildest cowboy on his ranch.

With a wary gaze to where the Murphy boy still hid, Cassidy came into the open. Rifle at the ready, she pointed to the black and white cow. "She's got a nick out of her left ear ... where my dog bit her."

Sure enough, just as she said, there was a notch. Course half the cows around sported a cut on their ears.

This was rough country. Wolves, cougars, coyotes any of them could have taken out a chunk.

Solomon looked up to where the boy hid. "You have any proof this is your cow?"

Ronan Murphy slid down the steep hill with Fisher scrambling behind him. He stopped on the opposite side of the creek. "We're missing a few. That's one of 'em."

Getting tired of having to settle their disputes, the judge glared at him. Although at sixteen, Ronan Murphy was more man than boy and the wild one of the Murphy clan.

"Son, I know you've been up before my court for more trouble than I could do in ten lifetimes. Why should I believe you?"

Ronan sneered at Cassidy. "Can't take the word of a Howard. You know they all lie."

Solomon caught the girl's rifle barrel on the rise and wrenched the gun from her hands. "There's not a cow alive that is worth a man's life."

Cassidy glared at him. "I heard you shot plenty who tried to steal your cattle."

"That was before we had law and order."

"There's no sheriff in Shirleyville."

"I'm a judge, and I have the … oh, why am I trying to explain it to a little girl. You just do as I say. I'll give this rifle to your father and let him deal with you."

The coy smile and sparkle in her eyes reminded him that Cassidy had her daddy tied and tossed. For a man with four daughters, Stephen had proven inept in dealing with half of them. The youngest and oldest seemed to be reasonable, but those two in the middle, well, the judge didn't envy Stephen the trouble they were bound for.

The judge threw the rifle to Matt. "Keep that until I try to figure out what to do with these two."

Catching it with one hand, Matt glared at Cassie. "Yes, sir. I'd say bending her over your knee and whooping her a few times sounds in order."

The judge grabbed Cassie's arm as she charged toward his foreman. Squirming like a wildcat, she pointed at Matt. "You just try it."

Matt winked at her.

"I agree with Matt." Ronan laughed. "I'd like to see that."

Tired of the ruckus, the judge shoved Cassie behind him. "If there's to be any whooping, it's going to be done by your fathers. And if I know Ben Murphy, I'd say your hide is about to be tanned."

Ronan backed away, the smile gone from his lips. After a quick glare at the girl, he faced the judge and shrugged. "It might be her cow, looks too scrawny to be one of ours."

Solomon stared at the boy. He'd caught Ronan in more than one lie before. "Good. That's progress. You willing to let her take this cow?"

The kid nodded. "I need to get home. My ma will be looking for me to come to breakfast. Sorry Judge." Ronan sent a scathing glare at the girl and mouthed, *I'll get you.*

The judge doubted it. Cassidy could take care of herself. Still, he'd make sure to tell her father and the boy's father what happened.

With his sternest look, Solomon pointed at each of the troublemakers. "I want you to tell your parents what went on here. The truth. And how you made me come out in the cold of morning to settle a dispute. I'll expect a good dinner from each of your families, and when I'm there, I *will* tell your parents what happened."

Neither of the kids looked the least bit remorseful. Ronan pointed toward his ranch. "Ma is cooking chicken today. I'll tell her to expect you if you want."

"That'd be good. I'll be at your cabin this afternoon." After making sure the two went their separate ways, the judge made his way to his horse. "Matt, if those two go at it again, shoot me."

His foreman chuckled. "You and me both. I'm hungry. I can smell George's flapjacks from here."

"The smell of burnt jacks do carry a long way on the wind. Let's get home, get warm, and eat our fill." On the way back, the judge had to laugh to himself. At least, he'd get two good meals out of the ordeal. Not that George wasn't a good chucker, but it'd been a long time since he'd tasted a woman's cooking. A fact that had prodded him to send that letter to the agency. Even now, he wavered between hoping it'd soon be answered or lost.

His mirth soured as he thought about the Murphy and Howard feud. The kids were getting older and like the morning's dealings showed, getting more dangerous. Cassidy wasn't the only one who knew how to shoot.

Solomon had hoped he'd spend his later years in peace. Those two families had spoiled that idea.

Ah, the dream he'd been in the middle of before Matt interrupted.

Clara.

"I miss you, gal."

^^^

Rachel Dowd plunged Larry's nightshirt into the water and rubbed vigorously to get the night stains and smell from his clothes. Perhaps it was because he was a twin that he wet his bed. Or maybe losing his father at such a young age. Still, his twin brother, Terry, had no problem in that area. They might be identical, but their personalities were night and day.

She stood and stretched her aching back. "Sarah, if you'll take the rest of the girls' things, I'll finish with the boys."

Her oldest daughter nodded. She was the quiet one. So much like her father. And so in need of her father.

Rachel glanced skyward and wondered if her husband was watching his family from his heavenly perch. That he'd died still came as a shock, and it'd been two years already. She held out the little nightshirt. Satisfied it was as clean as it was going to get, she handed it to Annie. "Hang this one up, please."

"Alright, Mama." With bright red hair and freckles to match, the little girl smiled wide and hung the nightshirt.

Rachel may have lost her husband, but she still had her children. All ten of them. For that she was thankful. She'd known several families who had all died from a fever. She surveyed the yard and her hard working and romping brood aged from twenty to four. She had just never counted on losing Frank in a freak accident. He was cutting down a rotted tree and a large branch had fallen and hit him in the head, killing him instantly.

After grabbing another shirt, Rachel was about to douse Robert's grass stained Sunday shirt in the water when she happened to look down the road and saw trouble coming. Fear trounced her peace. Frank had loved her and the children, but he'd not been good with the money. Add in a hard drought for the last two years and their farm was in trouble.

She set the shirt down and went to meet Mr. Hartsfield. No doubt, the banker had come to talk about her bills. He'd already warned that the bank would have to foreclose soon if things didn't turn around.

A darted look to the dry fields did little to alleviate her fears. She stopped and let the man walk the rest of the way toward her. Out of the corner of her eye, she felt relief as her oldest son, William, came from the fields to stand beside her.

Mr. Hartsfield took off his hat. "Mrs. Dowd, William." He sighed. "I had a meeting with the board. We're going to have to foreclose on the farm. You're too far behind. Whatever you get for the place won't even cover your debt." He paused, looked past her to the lively yard where her children romped. "We realize a widow in your situation can't take care of a family the size of yours. The town council has offered to help place some of your children in homes."

Rachel shoved a hand in her pocket. The letter had come yesterday. Until this moment, she'd not decided on her answer and had put off thinking about it. "No. I will not have my family torn apart. That we can't keep the farm is clear to me. I have made other arrangements." She stood tall and begged her confidence not to fail.

Mr. Hartsfield fiddled with his hat in his hands. "I am sorry, Mrs. Dowd. If there had been any other way,

I wouldn't have pressed the issue. It's out of my hands—"

"I understand." She didn't. Frank had poured himself into the land and the community. One lousy accident and all was lost to him. He wouldn't even be able to rest in peace knowing his family was taken care of and living on the farm he'd toiled so hard for.

"I pleaded with the board, but they want you out by the end of the month." He looked truly miserable.

Not willing to let him off easy, Rachel remained silent.

"Do you have somewhere to go?"

Feeling the paper in her hand, she nodded. "Yes." She didn't offer where and hoped this Judge Taggart would take in her and the children. His letter had agreed and offered an arranged marriage, but she'd never mentioned how many children. Montana would be a long ride. Too far to turn around and come back.

"Be out the end of the month, Mrs. Dowd." He sent a worried glance at William, and then turned and walked back to his waiting buggy and driver.

"Mother, do we have somewhere to go?"

She turned to her eldest. At twenty, he was a man. Should be on his own, but he stayed to help her out.

"That letter from Montana. Judge Taggart has agreed to marry me and give you children a home."

Concern worried his brows, so much like his father. "You don't know anything about him. And all the way to Montana Territory. Is there no other place?"

She put a hand to his cheek. "I don't want you to worry. We have no relatives, only one another. I will not have my family broken apart by well-meaning old biddies." Rachel had not realized how angry she'd become at the small town of Cadbury, Minnesota. But since the time of Frank's death, she'd been harangued by the older women telling her she needed to parcel out her children to those families in need of youngsters as a fever had taken so many five years ago.

Sadness tugged at his eyes. "I could get a job—"

The letter weighed heavily in her hand. "No, I've made up my mind." She glanced back at her brood. "I'll tell Sarah to watch the children and finish the wash. William, hitch up the buggy. We have things to attend to."

Her oldest took over and like a small army, the children marched to their oldest siblings commands, albeit, with a few looks her way and she pointing a warning finger in return.

First thing she needed to do was write an answer to the letter. She hoped Judge Solomon Taggart was a loving man. Although, by his stilted letter, he'd offered her a home but not love. Companionship. A marriage of convenience. A trade. She would be his wife, and he would provide for her and the children.

She finished her answer to his letter and sealed the envelope. Regret gnawed at her conscience. She had yet to reveal the number of her children. For all Judge Taggart thought, he was getting a wife at the cost of caring for a couple of children. Would he annul their agreement when he discovered she was bringing an army?

"Too late now." She grabbed her reticule, stuffed the few dollars they had, and left the house to find William. Today, she would arrange to sell what they couldn't take and seal their future. Sarah wouldn't be happy. She had that Adler boy interested in her. Yet, he never seemed quite the trustworthy type to Rachel. No, she and all her children would go.

A new life. She tried to keep the excitement in the forefront. To slip into the black abyss of leaving so many memories was too much. She'd not look back, only forward. For her children. They needed a future.

Rachel climbed into the wagon. She only needed to see her children happy and provided for and kept together. She wasn't looking for love or even friendship. Yes, she'd be a good wife for the judge. But only in return for his provision for her children.

Chapter 2

Judge Taggart splashed cold water on his face. He needed to be awake for the ride to the Murphy's for dinner. His stomach growled in complete irony to George's burnt offerings from below. Drying off, he spoke to the mirror. "Maybe the answer to that letter can't come soon enough."

He tilted his head and surveyed the spattering of silver in his hair. Frowning, he put on his tie and then jacket. Best to look all business when dealing with the feuding families. Even when going for a cordial dinner.

He avoided the picture on the dresser. What would Clara think? Easing his gaze to the photograph, he let out a sigh. "Nothing. You're not here any longer. You're in heaven with our daughter."

With purpose, he strode to the dresser and laid the picture face down. If Rachel answered his letter and agreed to be his bride, he'd have to put Clara from his mind. It wouldn't be fair to a new bride to compete with his dead wife.

He pulled out his pocket watch, verified the time, and stood straight. Time to go and see what excuses Ronan Murphy had come up with to tell his father.

20

They weren't bad people, but the valley and town were getting tired of putting up with the shenanigans of the feud.

Matt met him at the door. "Got your horse ready. Thought I'd ride with you. Heard there were bandits near the cutoff."

"No need to do that." The judge glanced at his foreman who was more like a son than a ranch hand. "But I appreciate the company." He strode to the black and mounted. "Easy, you big devil."

Matt held the bridle to keep the stallion in place. "Thought you'd want to ride him. I lunged him in the corral to get some of the wild out of him."

"Thanks, Matt." Gathering the reins, the judge gazed across his land, realizing he could only see a small portion of his holdings. When had life become so boring? He'd come to enjoy his warm bed all too much.

The judge nudged the horse into a lope. Like a coiled tiger, the animal sprung forward nearly unseating him. Shaking his head, the judge wondered when he'd grown so soft?

Matt caught up with him.

Trying to avoid the embarrassment of appearing the doddering old man, the judge patted his stomach. "I am hungry for Anna Murphy's bread. That woman can cook."

Matt grinned. "That she can."

"What are you grinning about?" The judge recalled the day he'd hauled Matt out of the street after he'd been thrown out of the saloon. Stone drunk and with not a penny in his pocket, the boy swung at him and caught him square on the nose. Blood streaming down his face, the judge had become so mad, he sentenced the young man to a month in jail. In that time, he grew to like the boy and hired him. That had been ten years ago, and Matt had worked his way up from rank ranch hand to foreman.

"Me, oh nothing. Thought I might go ahead and ride into town. Pick up the mail." Matt's face told what he was thinking.

"All right, so you think I'm an old fool for sending for a bride at my age."

Matt ran his mustang ahead, turned, and faced him. "No, sir. I think it's about time. You're not old. We're all pulling for you. Why, who knows, if it works out for you, some of us might just write a letter and get a bride for ourselves. Gets kind of lonely out here."

"That it does." The judge started to say more but shelved his thoughts for later. He wasn't at all sure he wanted a wife. Or more children. Seeing Cassidy and Ronan at each other's throats had about cured him of that.

Still, he had said in the letter that if the woman had children, it would be all right. After all, he had enough rooms in the big empty house to put up an army. He grunted an amused chuckle. She hadn't said how many, but he figured a couple. He could handle that. And at her age, they wouldn't be that young. "I'm hungry, let's get these horses moving."

They'd just rounded the bend in the road when the judge saw the youngest Murphy waiting for them. He sat hunched over, one leg resting over the saddle horn, while trying to roll a cigarette and pretend he was twenty-six and not sixteen.

"Your pa know you're smoking?"

Fumbling with the paper, it fell out of his hands. Ronan brushed the tobacco from his pants, sat up, and rode toward them. "Outlaws lives around here. Pa told me to come and make sure you were safe."

The judge wanted to say he knew that most of that trouble was in front of him, but withheld his jest, even

23

if it were true. "Thanks. Did you tell your pa what went on this morning?"

"Yes, sir."

Sliding a glance to the boy, the judge chuckled to himself, sure that Ronan's version would differ from the truth. One thing was certain; this feud was going to have to end before someone was killed.

The judge rode to the small cabin. How a man with four strapping sons could live in a place of such disrepair was hard to figure. Ben Murphy wasn't a lazy man per se, but he tended to throw his energy in the wrong place. Most of it in conflict with the Howards.

Anna Murphy stepped onto the porch. A small but pretty woman, she looked out of place in contrast to the yard strewn with broken tools. A smile lit her face. "Judge Taggart, hope you like fried chicken. Had Ronan kill a couple of my best hens."

The judge returned her smile. As long as he'd known the woman, he'd seen her put the guilt on those around her. Today, he figured it was in defense of the shabby state of her home. For that, the judge felt sorry for her. She was a proud woman with very little to be proud of.

In her day, Anna must have turned a line of heads. Her dark hair made quite a contrast to Ben's fiery red. Almost as if looking at them, one could get a precursor of what they were in for. The couple was like oil and water. She as soft spoken as a morning dove to Ben's bellowing, bullish behavior.

"I'm sure you made a wonderful dinner, Anna. Thanks for having me over."

"Ronan said you were coming." She glared at the boy, loading a burden of guilt on the lad.

The judge dismounted and handed the reins to Ronan just as Ben Murphy came from the barn.

The Irishman swaggered toward him as if he owned the world. "Howdy, Judge. Anna has dinner ready. Hope you're hungry."

One glance at the man was enough for the judge to see he was lying. Ben Murphy was as tight with his money and food as a starving dog standing guard over a caught rabbit. "I am." For some reason, he enjoyed needling Murphy. The man had been nothing but a thorn in the valley. He and his sons.

Anna shouted. "Ronan, hurry it up and get in here. This is your doing."

The boy rushed from the barn and brushed past him, scooted beyond his mother's reach, and stomped to the porch.

Contradicting his wife, Ben grabbed Ronan by the scruff of his shirt. "Boy, get your brothers," Ben grumbled, entered the cabin and threw his hat at the peg on the wall and missed.

The judge bent, picked it up, and placed it on the peg barely avoiding Ronan's mad dash outside. "How are things going, Ben? Your herd increasing?"

"Some, if you can keep them Howards from stealing any more of my cattle."

Anna set a plate of chicken on the table. "The girl brought the cow back. No sense causing more trouble between them than we already have."

So, Cassidy had been the one lying. He'd deal with her tomorrow. The judge noticed how tired Anna looked. Must be a tough road to be the voice of reason in a household of wild Irishmen.

Sounding like a herd of wild horses, Daniel, Adam, Thomas, and Ronan fought through the door and skittered to the table.

Anna pointed at the water bowl near the kitchen. "Boys, wash yourselves. We have a guest."

Grumbles and complaints echoed in the small cabin as they did their mother's bidding. Daniel finished first and took his seat next to the judge.

"Glad to see you, Judge."

Of all the Murphy men, Daniel was the most pleasant.

Thomas sat down and grinned. "That mail order bride come yet?"

"Thomas, need I remind you of your manners?" Anna sent a pained glance to the judge. "I am sorry for his behavior."

Not seeing any way to get out of the conversation, the judge placed the napkin in his lap and looked at the family. "I did send off for a bride. No, haven't had word of her accepting my proposal yet. Matt went into town to check the mail."

Anna passed the potatoes to him. "I hope you'll be happy, Judge."

"Thank you." He did too. Half the time he flipped from believing he was crazy, to daydreaming what it would be like to not be alone. Especially at night.

Ben pounded the butt end of his knife on the table. "Ronan tells me he had a run in with one of the Howard girls. Said she aimed a rifle at him. You going to set them straight?"

After chewing a piece of tough chicken, the judge set his gaze on the head of the Murphy household. "I was awakened early this morning to deal with your son and Cassidy. It's true she had a rifle. I took it from her. I'll handle the girl. I'm having dinner with her parents, tomorrow." After setting his fork down, the judge placed his hands on the table either side of his plate. "I want this feud business to end. The town is tired of it. Heaven knows I'm tired of dealing with your family and theirs. I'd hate to see a tragedy occur. We almost had one this morning. I don't want to think what might have happened if my men hadn't come along."

Ronan slammed his cup on the table. "I'd have settled it. No girl is going—"

The judge glared at the boy. "She had you treed like a howling cat. Cassidy is a sure shot. You'd best consider it the grace of God that you're not laid out for your funeral."

Ben erupted from his chair. "There'd be heck to pay if that ever happened. I—"

"You best get your affairs in order with the Howards. I'm in the mood to put the next offender in jail. And I'm not sure I'll let them out. Settle this feud now, or I will. It's bad enough I have to show up to negotiate peace between you and the Howards, but to make the town divide in half just because you won't agree to go to town on different days is ridiculous." The judge stood and ran a hand through his hair. "I'm at the end of my patience."

Anna put a hand on her husband's beefy arm. "Sit down, Ben."

Red-faced, Ben obeyed. "Only one way that feud is going to end, and that's if the Howards move on. Bad enough they're thieves, but they stink up the valley with those sheep."

Pointing a finger at the man, the judge struggled to rein in his own temper. "They have as much right to stay here as you do. Consider that. All of you." He took a breath to help settle his own anger and threw his napkin on the table. "Thanks for the dinner. Consider what I said. If nothing else, see that you don't go to town the same day as the Howards."

Ben swaggered to the door. "You know we always go on the first Saturday. Tell the Howards to stay home."

Ronan started to rise.

Anna snapped her fingers at him. Obediently, he sat back down. She went to her husband and stood next to him. "Judge, we'll stay away from them. I'll do my best to see that my boys obey."

"Thanks, Anna. Dinner was fine as always."

Ben nodded. "See you in town."

The judge grunted. It was the best he could do. He'd hoped the ornery Irishman would come to his senses, but he knew better. Ben and Stephen fought like two angry bulls whenever they were in eye's view of one another. "I'll see you, Saturday."

He left the Murphy's and prayed that the woman he'd corresponded with wouldn't choose that Saturday to come to town.

^^^

The next day, the judge rode to the Howards expecting a repeat of the one he'd had with the Murphys. This time it was Cassie who met him on the road and went to great lengths to explain she'd thought it was her cow until she got home and found their wandering bovine in the corral. The judge laughed as the girl begged him not to arrest and hang her for rustling.

The Howards had a cabin full of women. A sight cleaner and better smelling than the Murphy's for sure. Yet, the same underlying air of hate and anger tainted the atmosphere.

Stephen Howard was an affable man until the mention of the Murphys transformed him into an angry if not dangerous one. Nina, his wife, did her best to rein him in, but even she had little effect.

And then there was Cassidy. She was a spirited girl who was entering womanhood with a rifle and a man-sized grudge against the Murphys.

Finished with his second good meal in two days, the judge stood. "I want to thank you for the fine dinner. Stephen, I'd like to talk to you outside."

The man's grin faded. "If it's about the Murphys, you can say it here in front of my family."

"All right. The town and valley are tired of this feud. I'm tired of it. Your daughter nearly shot Ronan. I want it to end."

"That's not my call, Judge. Murphy started it, and he'll have to end it." He lit his pipe. "Best you take it up with Ben."

"I was there yesterday." Beyond exasperated, the judge threw a pleading glance at Nina. She looked away and began clearing the table.

Cassidy bolted out of her chair. "You need to run the Murphys out of the valley."

Neither parent sought to quiet the girl. The judge shot a glare at her. "They say the same about you. Maybe I should run the both of you out."

She started to respond when Stephen put a hand to her head and rubbed her blond hair. "Take care of the horses, Cass."

Her mouth opened but closed again after her father gently shoved her toward the door. Stephen shook his head. "A house full of girls and they're every bit as hard to handle as I imagine sons would be. That one, she's a pistol. Going to make some man trouble, blissful trouble, but trouble nonetheless."

Holding back a chuckle, the judge nodded. "That she will if she lives long enough. I'm warning you, what I saw on that ridge the other morning was a hint of the danger that's coming if this feud isn't resolved."

Stephen said nothing, just puffed on his pipe and avoided eye contact.

Having said what he could, the judge took his hat from the back of his chair and shrugged into his jacket. With one last attempt at peace, he turned and faced Stephen. "The Murphys will be in town Saturday. Why don't you and your family come in next week?"

Nina stopped her cleaning. "We need supplies, Judge, and I need to put some money in the bank. You tell the Murphys that we'll be in town and to stay clear of us."

The judge glared at them. "I'll be there, too. And I'll see that the first one to cause trouble goes to jail. That includes man, woman, boy, or girl."

Stephen walked to the door, opened it, and gestured it was time for him to leave. "Maybe Shirleyville needs a sheriff. Let him keep the peace."

"The town council is looking into it. Until we get one, I'll be the one to fill up that jail. Good day." The judge stormed out of the small cabin. Those families were headed for a showdown, and he wasn't at all sure the town was going to survive it.

As it was, every Saturday they drew lines in the sand. Half the town for the Murphys and the other half for the Howards. Fights broke out as storekeepers took sides. The judge doubted anyone even knew what the feud was about as the townsfolk changed sides with the month.

He mounted Big Sandy and galloped toward home. Saturday, he'd make sure to bring Matt and some of his best hands to town. Yet, even they got caught up in the rivalry. Odd thing was, one weekend some might be for the Murphys, and then the next time they'd be on the Howards side.

A cold breeze brought his attention to the northern sky. Dark clouds tumbled toward him, warning that change was coming. Quite possibly, in more ways than one. He thumped the letter in his pocket. Matt had given it to him yesterday. He'd still not read it. He'd planned to find a quiet place by the creek on the way back, read the letter, and see if his future included a woman or not.

Another look at the sky and he decided the weather wasn't going to pass by without a storm. He nudged the stallion and raced against the clouds, but his mind stayed on Rachel and the answer she'd sent.

He didn't know much about her. She was a few years younger than he was and did have children. She never said how many or what ages. Not that it really mattered. He'd run the ranch, and she'd run the household.

The coming storm heightened the lonely pit that hollowed out his stomach. He was plain tired of being by himself and grieving those who could not return. He'd finally faced the fact that he was alive and needed to go on living.

Why have a big ranch and no one to leave it to? He needed someone. Would he love her? He didn't think so. She didn't ask for love, only a place to live and provision for her and her children. Oh, she promised to do her wifely duties, but that's as far as she'd gone. Both of them had been looking for an arrangement between two people.

He frowned as the first few drops of rain hit. The judge spurred the horse on while his mind matched his horse's speed. Was he settling for less? He didn't have time to court a lady. No, if Rachel Dowd was agreeable to the arrangement, he'd go along.

The first cold drops of rain plunked hard on his hat. His thoughts turned to the feuding families. The reason he was about to be drenched. The judge spurred the horse on, and tried to turn his anger. It never did him well to be angry especially about things he couldn't control. He rode under the Rockin C gateway and into the yard just as the clouds let loose.

Matt opened the barn door, waved him in, and took his hat, pouring the rainwater from it. "The rain has finally come. That might ease the tension between the Murphys and Howards."

The judge slapped his coat to shake off some of the wet. "Doubt it. Those two families are filled with hate towards one another. Can't understand how they let their problems fester so that even their children are affected."

Matt took the horse and unsaddled it before sliding a grin his way. "Read that letter, yet?"

With a sigh, and regret that he'd told his foreman about the mail order bride, the judge patted his pocket and hoped the rain hadn't ruined the letter. "No, not yet."

"Want me to sit with you while you read it?"

With a rough laugh, he shook his head. "No, I'd rather be alone when I find out if I've been rejected or not." He pulled the envelope from his pocket, held it up, and eased over to a bale of hay.

He gently slipped his finger under the flap and broke the seal. With a wary gaze, he made sure no one was watching, and Matt was leading his horse to the stall. All alone, the judge opened the neatly folded yellow paper.

Dear Judge Taggart,

I accept your proposal. I am sure we can become a happy family. Thank you for allowing me and my children to come to Montana. I took the liberty of selling our farm and am using the money for tickets on the train and stagecoach. We should be there by the fifteenth of October.

Sincerely yours,

Rachel Dowd

His hands shook as he refolded the letter and slid it back in the envelope. Next Saturday, she'd be here.

Matt returned and hung the bridle in its place. "Well, do we need to clean up the ranch for your lady?"

Startled, the judge grinned. "Yes, we do. She'll be here a week from Saturday."

Matt let out a whoop and threw his hat in the air. "Glad for you, Judge."

A little annoyed that he couldn't stop a grin from spreading across his face, the judge nodded and hoped he'd be happy. Right now, his joy fled in the face of the guilt that had dogged him all day. What would Clara think?

And then there was George, his cook and house boy. The old chinaman might not take to a woman in the house. Especially if she wanted to cook. He sure didn't need another feud on his hands.

"Oh, Matt. I want you and some of the boys to go to town with me this Saturday. Both the Howards and Murphys will be there."

"How many? You know we're pushing a big portion of the herd up the valley."

"Maybe six if you can spare them. Might help if we have a little show of force to keep the fires between those families tamped down. Even the kids are ripe for a fight."

"Will do." His foreman stepped to the door and looked out. "Storm's blown over."

The judge ran a hand through his hair. If only that were true, he'd take rain any day over the storm that was going to converge on Shirleyville tomorrow.

Chapter 3

Early the next morning, the judge made sure he and his men were in town before the feuding families could get there. He sent two of his men to the general store, two to the livery, and two to the saloon.

Satisfied that he had the battlegrounds covered, he waited by the bank to warn Mr. Satchel that both families would be in town. Being the first half of the month, it should be a busy day and give cover to keep the families apart.

The judge eyed the bare street. Hardly anyone was moving, and it wasn't that early. Perhaps the weather yesterday was keeping people away. A worrying itch worked its way up his spine. He'd learned to heed that niggling feeling that warned all wasn't right.

"Morning, Judge. You have a worried look in your eye."

"Mr. Satchel, I was waiting for you. The Howards and Murphys are coming to town today."

"Figured they might. They both missed the last two weekends. I'll see that Charlie knows to keep an eye out for them." He checked his pocket watch. "Time to open up. You have any business today, Judge?"

"No, not today. Just trying to keep the peace."

"Council have any luck finding a sheriff, yet?"

With a resigned sigh, the judge shook his head. "I sent off a telegraph to Colorado. Hope to hear back soon."

After unlocking the door, the banker turned to him. "Hope we don't need a sheriff today, but I'm glad you and your men are in town."

The judge nodded. "We'll do what we can. It's getting harder each time they meet though."

"Yes it is. We ought to run them all out of the valley."

Dread tore at the judge's soul. He'd seen what happened when people took up sides and ultimatums were issued to stubborn men. "Hate for it to come to that, and the blood that would be spilled if it did. Let's hope it doesn't." A commotion at the end of town warned him the Murphys had arrived. Ben and the boys, men really, rode their mounts next to their mother in the wagon and nodded at him as they passed. Though polite enough, they all had the same steely glare for trouble in their eyes.

The judge walked to the edge of the boardwalk and up the street to meet them. "Ben, I meant what I said.

Any trouble and I'll have my men lock up you and your boys. Keep it peaceable today."

After stopping his horse, Ben spit a stream of tobacco to the ground. "We won't start anything. Right boys?"

His four sons answered.

"See that you don't. I meant what I said. You stay on the east side of town until I tell you. Then when the Howards are finished, I'll let you know. So do your drinking in the saloon now."

Ronan's horse reared. He reined it in a tight circle and stopped inches from the judge. "Not right that we have to go to the east side early. Not like the girls can go to the saloon."

His father grabbed the boy's reins. "You just do like the judge says. You're too young to drink anyway. Stay with Ma."

His eyes fiery, Ronan shook off his father's grip. "I'm old enough." The youngster didn't wait for more words, kicked his horse, and galloped away.

Anna Murphy sighed. "The land is too wild to hold onto these boys, Judge Taggart. Hope you'll be understanding."

"As long as they don't cause trouble with the Howards or anyone else, I won't arrest them."

Ben rode his horse beside the wagon to his wife. "I'll see to the livery. You do your banking and supply run. Afterwards, I'm going to take you to lunch at the café."

Anna blushed. "Ben, we shouldn't spend the money."

"Woman, you've got money to put in the bank. I want to take care of you the way you deserve." He bent to her and brushed a kiss on her cheek.

The judge left the two to work out their plans. He had to admit, it warmed his heart to see that Ben cared for his wife. That wasn't a sight he'd seen very often. Life in the west was hard, and hardest on women.

His thoughts jumped to Rachel Dowd. She was in Minnesota. How would she handle the west? Would she like him? Not like he was as kind and gentle as he used to be. The tough life on the range had knocked that out of him.

The light laughter of young women stole his attention. The Howards were now in town. Diverting his course, the judge walked to the other end of town and pointed to the west. "Murphys have the east until after lunch."

Stephen halted the wagon. "I've got business at the bank."

The judge looked the direction of the Murphys. More than likely, Ben would let Anna do their banking. "Take care of it and then get to the other side of town."

Nina put a hand on Stephen's arm. "I have supplies I need to get."

The judge nodded. "So do they. And they arrived in town first. When they're done, you can go to the mercantile. I'll ask Samuel if he might meet you at the feed store and take a list if you have one ready."

"Thank you, Judge."

Exasperated that the little town had to divide because of the feud, the judge threw them warning glares. "It would be a whole lot more peaceful if you two families could learn to get along."

Stephen slapped the reins, and the wagon moved away. "Not our doing, Judge."

Watching the man drive to the far end of town, the judge waited to make sure he stayed on the west side of the street. So far so good.

A quick look up the street showed the Murphy men had found the saloon.

The Howard girls would spend a lot of their day in Miss Holly's Dress Shop. Except for Cassidy, that little wildcat was already edging toward the livery. She loved horses more than sense.

Ignoring his own thirst, the judge walked toward the stable. Best send her away before Ronan saw her.

"Cassidy Howard, get on the west side of the street. Later in the day, you can get on the east and talk to Bill about his stock."

"Ah, Judge. I just want to see the horses. No crime in that is there?"

"None at all, but until your family can get along with the Murphys, you'll do as I say."

Kicking at the dirt, she frowned. "All right. Later then." She led her horse back to the western side of town and joined up with her sisters.

The judge rotated his shoulders to ease the aching knot lodged in the back of his neck. Trouble, he could feel it brewing like a storm. He gazed into the clear blue sky and hoped the day would remain just as clear of trouble.

A wagon loaded with miners rumbled down the street. The judge knew that by night most of the men would be laid out drunk and broke in the same wagon and headed back to the mines. They were a rough lot and added to the strain of the small town trying to grow into something decent.

The judge took a hard look at Shirleyville. He'd dreamed it would be a good place for families. Maybe someday it would. Right now, it grieved him to have to bring Rachel and her children to the town. There was a need for good women. Family types. He'd tried to run off the crooked gamblers and saloon girls, but the miners rioted. Seems the valley was steeped in trouble in one form or another.

The street began to look a little livelier. A couple of strangers rode by, and he made a point to check them out just in case. They didn't seem in any hurry or trouble. The mine owners had warned of a gang of outlaws terrorizing the valley. So far, they'd left the town alone.

The judge stopped at his courthouse, unlocked the door, and breathed in the musty smell of the law books. It reminded him of life in the university and how civilization should be. Good people obeying the laws and not engaging in crazy feuds or drunken brawls.

Picking up a book, he thumbed through the pages and thought back to better days. When he was on the bench in Memphis. The move west. Times when Clara and Shirley were alive. He'd forced them to move west with him. Shirley had loved it. Clara?

She'd gone along with him like she always had. At times, he thought her to be strong, but later he came to realize that she clung to him for strength. Afraid of losing him, she'd agreed to the trip west.

Clara got one year in the big house he had built for her, and then the fever took her. Took Shirley the next week and left him alone. Empty. That was eight years ago.

What would this Rachel think of his land? Of the empty acres and the only neighbors a far ride away? The nearest woman even farther.

He set the book down and sat behind his polished desk. His thoughts hung between the past and future, not finding peace in either one.

Shots rang out.

Anger boiled in his chest. That feud! He rose from the desk and started out of the office when he heard shouts and galloping horses.

A bullet plunked into the door just above his head, ducking inside, he saw four men gallop past. The judge recognized two of them as the strangers that had ridden by.

His gaze darted down the street. Mr. Satchel, waved a pistol in the air and ran toward him, shouting, "Bank's been robbed."

The judge dodged back inside his courtroom and brought out his rifle. "Get up a posse."

Mr. Satchel grabbed his arm. "Anna Murphy and Stephen Howard were shot. I think they're dead."

"Get the doc and take him down there. I'll get the posse." The judge prayed for them. He didn't want more killing, and neither of those families would let it go. Somehow, they'd accuse each other for the deaths.

Sure enough, the Murphy men came out of the saloon at a dead run.

The judge stared at the elder Murphy and remembered the tender moments he'd had with his wife. He grabbed the man by the arm and spoke softly.

"Ben, your wife was shot. You and your boys might want to go to the bank first."

The big man's face went white. He nodded, waved his boys to follow, and ran toward the bank.

The judge left one of his men in town with instructions to take care of the bank and the injured.

Matt rode up, leading his horse. "We're ready. Black Jack was in the saloon. He can track a snowflake in a blizzard."

The judge mounted, waved his rifle in the air, and swore in the posse. "Let's go. I'll not put up with this lawlessness." He fired a shot and they rode after the gang. The outlaws had been getting bolder, but today was the first time they'd come into town to do their dirty work.

The posse followed the trail until it disappeared in the rocks where the badlands ate up the grass with chunks of jagged rocks.

Matt knelt beside Black Jack, traced a finger in the dirt, and then stood. "We can't tell nothing by the tracks. Most of them are from buffalo." He pointed toward the rocky chasm. "We'd need an army to search them out. They could be sitting on any bluff and pick us off."

Tired beyond his years, the judge nodded. "Let's get back to town." He dreaded what he'd find and hoped the feuding families weren't at each other's throats. The ride back was quiet with the silence of defeat.

It was nearly dark by the time they rode back to town. No shots or shouting was a good sign. Then again, the air of death hung over the town like a black shroud. Two wagons were outside the doctor's office. Muphys one, Howards the other. Uncharacteristically, side by side.

No angry words littered the air. Only sorrow and the silence of death. The judge rode to the nearest wagon, the Murphys'. A body, covered by a blanket told the story. Ben sat red-faced and bleary eyed in the wagon next to his wife's body.

"I'm sorry, Ben."

"Did you get them?" The man's voice was flat.

"No. They disappeared past the Prouty spread into the badlands."

Ronan mounted his horse. "When are we going to look for them?"

Ben grabbed his son's arm. "Not now, boy. We got your ma to tend to."

Tears moistened Ronan's eyes. Though he didn't say anything, neither did he ride off.

The judge looked to the other wagon. Nina Howard was in the back of it, holding the body of her husband.

Doc Hasbro came out of his office. "Judge." He waved him aside and whispered. "Stephen was dead. I tried to save Anna, but she'd lost too much blood. Charlie is resting, just a wound in his arm. Mr. Satchel said they got all the money."

Grimacing, the judge nodded that he'd heard. "Anyone else hurt?"

"No. Just the three in the bank." The doc looked at the posse. "Any of your men injured?"

"No. Just tired."

Doc nodded toward the wagons. "Jake Deeds tried to get them to let him take care of the bodies at the funeral parlor, but the families didn't want either of their loved ones near the other."

The judge rubbed his chin. "The women are going to need the most help. I'll talk to Mrs. Howard and her daughters."

"I tried that. Cassidy told me to get away."

"I'll handle the families."

The judge walked to the Howard wagon. "Nina, sorry for your loss. Let us help you. Jake can lay out the body, and we can have the funeral in the cemetery."

She didn't look up, just hugged her husband's head to her.

Cassidy came up to him. "We'll take care of our own."

"You sound like your father, girl. And that's admirable. But there comes a time when it's wise to accept help from others. This is one of those times."

Aileen, the oldest daughter, came to him. "We'll get him ready at home. Maybe you and Jake can come by tomorrow. Mama wants him buried by the church next week."

"We'll do that. I'll have my foreman and a couple of men stop by in the morning to help."

She put a delicate hand on his arm. "Would you come, too? It would mean a lot to us. Papa thought highly of you."

"Sure. I'll be by in the morning."

Chapter 6

Rachel Dowd leaned her head against the thin cushion of the stagecoach. Judge Solomon Taggart had spared no expense on her. Even though she'd written that she had funds for the fares, he'd wired her a generous sum of money so that she had enough for all their tickets and more.

She glanced out the window at the rolling hills and grass of Montana. Perhaps if the fields on her small farm in Minnesota had sprouted grass instead of rocks, Frank wouldn't have worked himself so hard.

She sighed. No sense in thinking of the past. She and her children were now committed to a man she knew only by correspondence. While the judge seemed to be considerate, how could one truly know about a man unless you were with him? Soon, she'd find out if she had chosen wisely or foolishly. Unfortunately, there would be no going back.

Larry squirmed beside her. "I want to ride on top with the big boys."

She scooped the little boy into her embrace. Whatever else happened, she had her children. There had been no choice for her. All the other men looking for a bride her age requested no children. Only the judge had agreed. And even then, he hadn't known the extent of that agreement.

"Mama, I'm tired of sitting. I liked the train better."

"Oh, is that so." She sent an amused glance to the one passenger who was not one of her children. "We should be to Shirelyville, soon. We'll meet a very important man there."

"Our Father?"

The gentleman across from her opened his eyes wide.

She tried to ignore his intense stare and poured her attention on her son. "We shall see. You just do what I tell you to do. And when we get off the stagecoach, I am telling you to do just as William says."

His little face mushed into a frown. "Yes, Mama."

Rachel eased back in her seat again, her heart paining in sorrow that the young ones had so little time with Frank. She rested her head against the thin cushion and tried to think of good times. The murmurs of her children reminding her that she needed to soak up the peace while she could. Once they met Judge Taggart, her children would need her even more. She wasn't sure what the judge would think of her and her brood. She prayed he wouldn't send her packing.

Judge Taggart. What did he want her to call him? He'd signed all his letters the same. Of course, there had only been three of them. Was she to call him Judge? Not very romantic. A chorus of laughing children caused her to smile. With that army, there was little chance for romance.

Two lonely people who needed companionship, wasn't that what she'd agreed to? Judge Taggart wanted a family to share his house and ranch. Never a mention of love. She tugged at the ring on her finger. She'd have to remember to remove it before they reached Shirleyville. Frank, he'd been her love. Rachel had come to the conclusion he'd been her one and only. From here on out, it was merely a matter of convenience.

Tears stung her eyes, catching her off guard. After two years, she'd thought her time of grieving was over. She didn't have time to spend pining over a man in a pine box. The accident had taken him and left her alone with ten children to care and provide for.

"Impossible." Mrs. Bates had declared and offered to take the six youngest to an orphanage.

Even in her darkest hour, Rachel had known that she would keep all of her children. All were dear to her heart. Each one a love note of remembrance of Frank's love for her.

But what would that be like after she married another man? Shivers traced up her spine. Judge Taggart, what would he be like? Would they sleep in the same bed? He would expect it. He was a man.

Her cheeks grew hot. She shot a glance to the man in the coach and then to her twins, her youngest. She would always be a mother first. The judge may be expecting a wife, but that would take time. He'd best know that.

Or else?

Her silent bravado melted before the heat of reality. She had nowhere else to go. No way to make enough money to support her family. No, she was trapped in this marriage of convenience. Empty bed or not.

Rachel closed her eyes and sent up a quick prayer that the judge would be a kind man, good to her children, and above all else, patient with her.

^^^

The judge took great pains to shave close, leaving his mustache, but trimming his sideburns. He put on his Sunday best for the funerals and for later when he would pick Rachel up from the train station.

He was driving the carriage, while Matt was bringing the wagon to load her belongings. Only proper that he should begin their courting in a fancy rig. Alone. He figured the children could ride with Matt. Besides, his foreman was good with kids.

Once outside, he saw that Matt was ready and waiting. He was a good man. "We better get to town early. I don't think the Murphys and Howards will still be fighting their feud during the funerals. Still, I hate that Reverend Sullivan couldn't be here. He has a way of calming them down. Can't believe Jake made the funerals so close to one another."

Matt held the reins. "From what I heard, he tried to put them on different days. The families wouldn't hear of it and forced him to do the two funerals on the same day. I sent Yates and Barrows to town just in case we need them."

The judge settled in his buggy. "Good idea. Although, I can't imagine Nina and Ben would allow their children to go at each other's throats during this sad time."

Matt shook his head. "I heard they got into a shouting match at the undertaker's."

That was something the judge didn't need on the day he was to pick up his bride. What was it going to take to settle those two families down?

Gazing toward town, Matt shrugged. "The storeowners are getting tired of accommodating those two families."

"So am I. I'm not going to have time to be dragged into their quarrels."

Chuckling, Matt handed him the reins. "No, I'd say you'll be a mite busy. We're all pulling for your happiness with this woman, Judge."

"Thanks. Appreciate that." He looked back at the big lonely house. Probably the last time it'd be quiet. Of course, he really didn't know how old Rachel's children were. He'd not asked, and she'd not said. He snapped the reins. Whatever was going to be, waited for him in town.

Despite the rain last night, the day was sunny and warm. A nice day to bring a new prospective bride to the ranch. Topping the hill, the judge scanned the town.

He drew in a breath and wondered if the icy river shooting through his veins was because of Rachel or the funerals for Stephen Howard and Anna Murphy.

The town looked peaceful enough, but the feeling of unrest wouldn't leave him. Even the sturdy bay harnessed to the buggy seemed on edge as if a grizzly lurked in the area. Matt drove up beside him.

"Trouble?"

"No, none that I see." The judge glanced to the cemetery. Coming from opposite ends of town, two wagons neared the grassy knoll. "Then again, we might be early."

Matt whistled. "You might be right. I thought the undertaker made the funerals an hour apart."

"He did." Not wanting to wait for the families to get into an argument, the judge slapped the reins and drove to the cemetery. He halted the buggy, jumped out, and strode to the undertaker.

"Jake, you have everything you need?"

"Yes, sir." The man always reminded him of President Lincoln. Tall, bearded, and continually solemn.

"Which family are you doing first?"

Jake pointed at the Murphy wagon just driving down the lane and ahead of the Howards by half a mile. "Anna Murphy, rest her soul." He turned his lanky frame toward the judge. "They won the coin toss, but seeing the Howard wagon coming in, I have to say I'm relieved you're here."

The judge smoothed out the wrinkles on his suit coat. When officiating, he liked to look his best and felt it added an air of integrity if not power when he sought to dispense justice. He glanced at the undertaker. "I don't think there will trouble. Not in this time of grieving."

Jake's wary gaze said different.

The judge hoped there wouldn't trouble. He strode to Ben Murphy and clapped a sympathetic hand on the man's shoulder. "Sorry for your grief, Ben. I know how you're feeling."

"Thanks, Judge." Ben glanced up at him with red eyes. "I can't believe she's gone. After, well, after today, my boys and I want to help you find the ones that did it."

"Of course, there'll be time for that later. Right now, your boys need you. Keep a steady hand on them that they don't go after the gang. Hate to see you lose anymore over the matter."

Ben shot a look at Ronan. "I think you're right. After that rain last night, the lower pasture will be flooded. I'll keep them busy moving the herd."

The undertaker cleared his throat. "Shall we begin?"

Ben nodded. "Boys, carry your mother." His stern voice cracked.

Looking like stepping-stones, Daniel, Adam, Thomas, and Ronan split up and carried the pine casket to the gravesite. Daniel, the oldest looked most like his mother. Adam and Thomas sporting their red hair favored their father. Ronan was a mixture but seemed to contain all the wild of both sides of the family.

They walked to a grave dug on the west side of the lone oak in the middle of the cemetery and laid the box next to it.

"Papa gets the west side!" Cassidy broke free from her mother and sisters and ran to the edge of the procession.

The judge turned and lowered one of his famous scathing stares at her.

She wasn't fazed one bit. Although dressed like a lady in pink, her demeanor had a distinct emphasis on the *mean*. With brows furrowed, she pointed. "That's my papa's grave. He loved sunsets."

Ronan bristled like a young porcupine. "So did our Ma."

Fearing an uprising, the judge moved between the two rivals. "Jake, what was decided?"

Stove-top hat in place, Jake held up his Bible. "Ben Murphy, you said it didn't matter where the grave was as long as it was in the shade of the oak. Being it's the only tree in the cemetery, I put one on the east of the tree and one on the west. Would it be agreeable to bury Anna on the east side?"

With hat in hand, the head of the Murphy clan eyed his boys. "No, no she enjoyed watching the sun slide its way to night. She'd want the west side."

Shouts of agreement arose from his sons.

Sighing, the judge looked around to see where Matt was and spotted him at the edge of the road. Waving for him to come, the judge faced the Murphys. "You got to go first, why don't you let the ladies have the west side?"

Ben shook his head. "We're already here. Can't you just let her rest in peace?"

The answer came in the form of a dirt clod, mud really, aimed perfectly at Ronan's white shirt. Splat.

Before the judge could turn to stop an escalation, Ronan scooped a muddy handful and threw it at Cassidy, leaving a brown splotch on her pink dress.

More shouts, more clods, and soon the cemetery and its inhabitants were doing anything but resting in peace.

Sick and tired of the feud between these two families, the judge pulled out his pistol and fired into the air. Mud balls flew through the air, hitting him from both sides and soiling his jacket and shirt. How was he going to explain that to his intended?

Matt ran past him, went to tackle Cassidy but Bridgett, the Howards second oldest daughter, tripped him.

Bridgett stormed past Matt and faced Ben. "After all the hardship you have caused us, I think the least you could do would be to honor our wishes."

Ben growled. "Hardship is nothing compared to what you and your clan of sheepherders have done to us and this valley. It would be best if you left. All you Howards."

Nina Howard gently tugged on Bridgett's arm. "Come back and help me keep the girls safe. Looking tired, Nina pointed at the tree. "Truth is, Stephen wouldn't care which side of the tree he was buried on. Girls put those dirt clods down."

Not to be outdone, Ben puffed out his chest and roared at his boys. "Drop your weapons. Let the women have their way. Ma liked sunrises and sunsets." He poked Jake in the chest. "You just make sure she can't see *his* grave."

Nodding, Jake walked around the tree to the other grave. "Shall we do this then?"

Cassidy kicked at the clods littering the ground. "We don't want this mess on our Papa's grave site. You keep this one, and we'll take the east."

More shouts filled the air.

Angrier than he'd been in some time, well, maybe in the last five minutes, again the judge shot his gun into the air. "Stop it! This is how it will be. Ben, you bury Anna on the west side and Nina, you bury Stephen on the east side. Now clear out to your appropriate corners. I don't want to hear one word out of either side."

Cassidy opened her mouth, but when he pointed at her, she shut her mouth and dropped the clod in her hand.

The judge brushed his vest, but the dirt stains remained. "Get on with it, Jake, before we need to dig another hole."

Thirty minutes later, Anna Murphy and Stephen Howard lay peacefully in their graves under the lone oak tree. But by the grumbles, frowns, and angry stares, there'd be no peace between the two families. And that meant no peace for the town, the valley, or him.

He pulled out his pocket watch. The stagecoach should be pulling into Shirleyville any time now. The judge put away the idea he'd have time to visit Clara's grave. He tapped Matt on the shoulder. "Take over for me and make sure the families leave town."

His foreman grinned. "Sure will. I'll drive by the depot to take the trunks and children to the ranch."

The judge nodded but had already moved on; his mind on Rachel Dowd. What would she think of him? He glanced at his jacket and the muddy stains. Then he looked at the small town.

Shirleyville was growing, but it lacked much of what the civilized part of the United States had. There wasn't a school. No sheriff. There were two saloons that sported a large share of trouble on any given night. The few women in town belonged to the saloons. Well, there was Dolly who ran the dress shop. Mrs. Satchel, the banker's wife. Maybe a trickling of others.

Not that he believed Rachel would spend much time in town, but he did want her to like her new home and town. Dust rose in the east. The stage was coming. With a grimace, the judge got in the carriage and flicked the reins. The least he could do was to be there before she got out of the coach.

Chapter 7

Rachel shuddered as the rocking coach came to a halt. She'd soon meet the man she'd agreed to marry. She should have asked for more time to get to know him. Then again, it wasn't like she had the time or more than one choice.

Judge Solomon Taggart had been the only man to answer her well thought out advertisement. And she'd yet to tell him about her children. She closed her eyes in silent prayer. Her eyes flew open when Larry crawled over her and hung out the window.

Shouts of Mama echoed in and atop the stagecoach. What was the judge going to think? She took hold of the two youngest, Larry and Terry. "Children I want you to take the hand of your partner sibling. She poked her head out the window. "William, see to the boys and get them down safely, please. Sarah take care of the girls. Remember, you all must be on your best behavior."

Larry turned and looked up at her. "So's the big judge doesn't put us in jail?"

She cupped his angelic face and smiled. "No, he isn't going to put you in jail. He's a good man. I want him to like us."

Kathleen squirmed. "If he doesn't, is that when we go to jail?"

"No, darling. Judge Solomon is not going to put us in jail."

Ten-year-old Penelope gasped. "Is he going to cut us in two like the Solomon in the Bible?"

Rachel knelt and gathered her brood in her arms. "Little ones, the judge is a good man and has promised to take care of us. I don't want anyone to be afraid."

William cleared his throat and opened her door. "Time to go." He picked up Larry as the boy dashed by.

Sarah exited and kept the girls in line. "We've got the children. You go out first and meet him."

Rachel didn't know whether to cry or laugh at the sight of her brood. She nodded, picked up her satchel and walked toward the boardwalk.

The stage driver grinned. "Pleasure having you aboard, Ma'am." He held her elbow and steadied her as she stepped up.

Her gaze landed on the one man who could be the judge. He was neatly dressed except stains marked his jacket and shirt. At least, he was smiling.

"Rachel Dowd?" He strode to her and held out his hand.

Not sure if she should shake his or merely hold her hand out, Rachel clumsily bumped her hand into his. "Y-es. Judge Solomon Taggart?" She still had no idea what to call him.

"I have my carriage here. My foreman will take your bags and children." He looked around her with a puzzled frown.

Rachel turned. None of her children had come forward. Instead, they remained on the other side of the coach. "I am sorry. For some reason, they stayed by the coach. William, bring the children."

"Oh? Were they opposed—"

"No, no. Nothing like that. Just shy."

The echoes of her herd made their presence known as they came from behind the stage, one by one.

The judge gave her a weak smile. "Which ones are yours?"

Rachel held out her arms, and her gaggle of children ran to her. "All of them."

"All?"

"All, ten of them." Seeing the shock on his face, Rachel stammered. "Th-three of them are nearly grown." She gazed at the man and prayed he wasn't going to turn her away.

He smiled weakly. "Well, I did say children were acceptable. Good thing I have a large house with plenty of rooms." He pointed to a fancy carriage. "I wanted to drive you home alone. Give us a chance to get to know one another. My foreman, Matt Stearns, has the wagon and will follow with your belongings and children."

She nodded. "William, will you take the twins." She clapped her hands to establish control. "Two by two, children. You will go to that wagon by the alley and let Judge Taggart's foreman drive you to our new home."

Her voice caught when she said the last word. Would it ever feel like home? Would her children feel at home? She glanced at the judge. Would they ever be a family?

"Shall we go?" The judge smiled, a bit warmly now.

"Yes." Her heart thumped so loud she feared he would hear it. What had she done? She prayed he was a good man. Would he be kind to her children. To her.

He guided her down the step and helped her climb into the carriage. She'd never ridden in one so fine. It occurred to her that perhaps she'd chosen a man of means. While important, she swept the thought aside and continued to pray that he would be good. Money didn't buy everything.

And then there was the matter of the dirt on his jacket. Her first thoughts about his being wealthy evaporated. Then again, he was a judge. Or had been one.

The carriage swayed as he took his seat.

Instinctively, she scooted away from him although there wasn't far to go.

"Rachel, you don't mind me calling you by your first name, do you?"

"That's fine." She swallowed her fears. "And you. What shall I call you?"

He half-snorted. "Most people call me the judge. Even my ranch hands. My Christian name is Solomon. I guess that will do." He faced her. "Might have to call me twice. Been some years since anyone used my first name."

Sensing an uneasiness, she touched his arm. "If you'd rather I didn't—"

"No. It's my name."

She nodded slightly. "All right. Solomon." She paused. "Would it be acceptable for me to call you Sol?"

The judge relaxed. "That would be fine. I like that."

"Very well, Sol. Let's get acquainted while we're alone." She stopped talking. It would serve her right if he returned her to Minnesota because she'd failed to tell him she had ten children.

He laughed. A loud free laugh. "I think you're right, Rachel. It's going to take me some time just to learn all the children's names."

^^^

Sol. Well, that would take him some getting used to. Clara had lovingly called Solomon. His ranch hands, the townspeople, everyone else called him Judge. Rachel's perfume drifted to him, smelling sweet and holding the promise that he was in the presence of a lady.

71

He glanced at her. She sat stiff, eyes straight ahead. She was a handsome woman. Her hair was dark but graced with strands of silver. Slim but shapely. Seeing her in town, he would have been attracted to her. Now, he was committed to marrying her.

"Hope you like Montana."

She startled slightly and looked at him. "I was caught in the beauty of your country. So, open, the rolling hills and mountains in the distance. It is beautiful."

So was she. He hadn't planned on being taken in by her looks. In fact, he'd worried about what he was getting. Thoughts of a weighty woman with a sour face had antagonized his thoughts. He couldn't have been more pleased.

"The winters are hard."

She nodded. "I understand that. Minnesota is cold, too. We'll survive. We always do." She clutched her reticule close to her. "I am hoping that the children can keep their father's name."

The children. He'd given them little thought. True, she hadn't told him names or ages. And that there were ten of them had come as quite a shock. A few of them looked grown. He put his hand on hers. "That would be fine with me. I'll treat them all well. I'm prepared to make them heirs."

She lowered her head and cried quietly. After a time, she wiped her eyes and looked at him. "Thank you. I can see you are a good man. I pledge to be a good wife."

"Rachel, you don't need to fear me." He happened to catch site of some of the dirt stains on his jacket. He futilely brushed at one, shook his head, and grinned at her weakly. "I am sorry about my appearance. I had to dole out some justice between two feuding families, and I'm afraid I was awarded with dirt clods. Mud really as it rained last night."

A smile tweaked her lips. "A dirt fight. And here I thought the Wild West suffered from gunfights."

Thinking of the Murphys and Howards resurrected his anger. "I'm at my wits end about the feud. The town has to divide itself whenever they come in. And this morning, we were burying one from each side. You'd think they could be solemn and respectful during a funeral."

Her expression turned to sorrow. "That does seem hard to believe, but the stains on your jacket are evidence."

"I'm going to have to meet with them in the morning. The town wants a solution."

"Pray."

He glanced at her.

She met his gaze. "Your name is Solomon. Pray for the Lord to give you the answer. The wisdom. He will."

"You say that as if you mean it."

She held her head high. "I am not a saint, but I have seen the Lord work on my behalf during my times of need. Of which there have plenty since my husband was taken from me." She lowered her eyes for a moment. "A tree limb fell on him and killed him instantly. We were forced to sell our farm."

"I'm sorry. Perhaps I can look into—"

"No." She held a gloved hand out. "That's the past. My children and I are here to make a new life. With you, if you'll have us."

He pulled the reins halting the carriage. "Rachel, my word is good. After we get to know one another and you agree, I'll marry you." He wanted to add more. To tell her he wished they could have more than a marriage of convenience. But then again, he'd just met her.

And there was Clara. The memory of her lingered and even now was at odds with the feelings he was already experiencing with Rachel. He'd not planned to like her so quickly. *Like?* He'd taken one look at her and felt as if he'd known her for years. He couldn't explain it and didn't want to.

Rachel sat in silence for an awkward moment. Then she nodded. "I came to marry you. My word is also good. Whenever you feel it is proper, I am ready."

Surprised by her candor, he nodded, slapped the reins, and started the horse toward home. He'd thought about showing her his favorite place. But now, he only wanted to get home. Although with the invasion of a woman and ten children, it was hardly going to feel like what he'd grown used to. He doubted there'd be any quiet nights or days.

"Very well, let's say the last of the month. That will give us a few weeks to get to know one another." He clicked to the horse to keep it steady. "There are lots of rooms in the house, but I can stay in the bunkhouse if that would make you feel more at ease. I like to see that things are done according to principle."

She dabbed her eyes with a lacey handkerchief. "Thank you. I do value the time to get to know you, but I worried about the appearance of impropriety. Although, I should be the one moving to town."

He shook his head. "The town's not quite tame enough yet. We've sent off for a sheriff, but right now, it's a wild mining town. And then there's the feud. It's bad enough the families are at each other, but the town takes sides, and it leads to fights."

A gunshot shattered the peaceful scene. The judge looked to the west and saw a rider coming at breakneck speed while another from the opposite side raced toward them.

Chapter 8

Rachel put a hand to her chest and begged her heart to keep beating. She also scooted closer to the judge. She'd not been around guns much, but she knew what she was hearing. Another gunshot blasted the quiet.

She grabbed his arm. "My children!"

"They're fine. Nothing to worry about." He halted the horse and waited for the riders to reach them.

"Put your guns away. What is it now? How did you even have time to get into trouble with the funeral this morning?"

A wild girl with a mane of blond hair slid her horse to a stop. She lowered her rifle and then pointed at a handsome young man. "He and his lowlife family are threatening our sheep."

Sol groaned as he turned to face the boy. "That true Ronan?"

The girl glared at the boy. "Not just threatening. Yesterday, we caught them by the creek with those smelly animals. You know they ruin the grass."

Sol grunted an uh-oh. "I'm sorry, Ronan. In all the confusion and with the loss of your mother, I forgot to tell you Murphys that I agreed to let the Howards water their sheep at my creek."

The boy put his pistol in the holster. "How are we going to know when they're at the creek? Our cattle get thirsty and won't drink after the smelly critters dirty the water hole."

Waving a hand, Sol motioned for them to come together on his side of the wagon. "We're going to settle this. Once and for all." He grasped Rachel's hand. "This is my wife to be, and we're on our way home. Tomorrow morning, I want both of your families at the courthouse. This feud is ending."

The girl snorted. "They started—"

"That's enough, Cassidy. I'm stopping it. Now, can I trust the two of you to get home without killing each other?"

They both answered with a scowl.

Sol waved them away. "Get home, then." He turned to Rachel and smiled reassuringly. "That's what we're doing."

The two young tornadoes galloped away taking the air with them. Rachel concentrated on making her breathing return to normal. "Sol, what are you going to do? They are so angry."

"The boy is Ronan Murphy. He's the youngest of the clan and the wildest. He's got three brothers, Daniel, Adam, and Thomas. Their father is Ben Murphy, and when you meet that bear, you'll see where they get their unruliness. The other family is the Howards. A family of girls. Cassidy is number three and the wildest of her family. Aileen is the oldest daughter and gentle as a deer. The next one is Bridgett. She's a siren and drives men crazy. The youngest is Darby, who fortunately takes after Aileen. Their mother, Nina Howard is a nice woman but strong, and trust me, you wouldn't want to cross her."

Rachel nodded as she took in the information. "So, basically, you have a family of men and a family of women, and they have a wicked feud between them?"

Sol slapped the reins. "That's about it. Last week, bank robbers killed Mrs. Murphy and Mr. Howard. We had the funerals this morning."

"Oh dear. I don't envy you. Then again, your name is Solomon. You're going to need wisdom. What is the feud about?"

He shook his head. "No one knows. I doubt if the families even know. The gossip is that the two men were partners in a mine." Sol faced her. "I think it's deeper than that. I've dispensed justice for some time and usually when there's a deep-hatred between two men, it involves a woman."

Rachel's cheeks grew hot. However, from anger or embarrassment, she wasn't sure as both emotions rose up inside her. She licked her lips and thought carefully about how she should respond. She glanced at him, and her anger grew. The man wasn't even waiting for her to speak.

He'd stated the insult as if it were a fact that women were behind man's troubles. "Sol, am I to believe that you think women are at the heart of the trouble between men?"

"What?" He stared at her as if she'd suddenly appeared.

"You said the feud was caused by a woman."

His brows furrowed. "No one knows. It's just that it has been my experience that more men have come to blows over a woman than anything else."

She folded her arms. "I don't agree." She darted a glare at him and became angry all over again at the look of confusion on his face. He truly did not understand what an insult he'd leveled at her and half the earth's population.

Somehow, in all the turmoil in her mind, she noticed his rugged face, dark hair, and blue eyes. To stop her fluttering heart, she looked ahead at the low rolling hills. "Perhaps, if women weren't looked upon as beneath men and regarded as objects, men wouldn't fight over us as if we were but another piece of property."

"Whoa." The horse slowed. Sol grinned. "Not you horse." He clicked to urge the horse forward. "I'm sorry if you get the idea that's how I view women or you. I didn't ask you out here, or to marry me, because I needed another item. I asked you here because I was lonely and wanted to share my life with a woman."

Rachel bit back her tears. Why had she become so angry? The answer came to her as she looked at the grassy hills. She had been forced to sell the farm. As a woman, she couldn't own property or have a business. If the judge hadn't agreed to send for her, she could have lost her youngest children.

She gathered her composure. "I'm sorry. The long day of traveling has worn me out and made me a little irritable. I won't let it happen again." She prayed he'd not send her back.

The carriage stopped.

She flinched. Was he turning around? Changing his mind?

"Rachel, you can trust me. I meant with all my heart that I would protect and provide for you and your children. All ten of them." He took her hand. "I am sorry if you've been hurt."

Tears wetted her cheeks. Embarrassed, she looked away and choked back her sobs as she fought to regain her composure. She did not want him to see her as weak, or as someone he could rule and run over.

He didn't say anything. Nor did he move the horse on.

When she was sure her voice would hold, she faced forward. "I'm ready. I don't want the children to worry."

He put a hand on hers. "You can trust me, Rachel. I won't do anything to hurt you, or your children."

The warmth from his hand seeped into hers. She longed to believe him.

He slapped the reins. "Let's go, horse."

He didn't say anything else. Yet the silence between them was warm, like the feeling she still had on her hand where his had rested. Perhaps she could trust him.

^^^

The judge rode on in silence. What had he done? He should have known that this woman would come with troubles of her own. She didn't seem to trust men. Would he be able to win her over? Did he want to?

No, this letting another woman enter his life may not have been a good idea. He'd thought the lonely life was hard. Now, he had to share his life with another person. One who may or may not want to share herself with him. Had she only wanted a home for her children?

And that was another thing. Ten kids! How was that going to work out? It'd take him a month to learn their names. Already, the oldest son, William, looked at him as a rival. *What have I done, Clara?*

And that brought up another problem. Could he give his heart to another woman? He'd loved Clara with all he had, and he'd buried a big chunk of his heart when she died. His thoughts drifted to Ben Murphy and Nina Howard and cringed at the pain they must be going through. And Rachel. She'd lost her husband.

He glanced heavenward and said a silent prayer. *Lord, this life sure has its share of heartache. Hope You're watching and will help sort things out down here. Preacher says You do. Sometimes, I'm not so sure. You could have warned me about the ten children. Not sure how that's going to play out on my ranch.*

He stopped his prayer as he turned on the road to the ranch. "The Rockin' C is the biggest ranch in the valley. I helped drive a herd of longhorns to the valley ten years ago. I found gold on my property. I'm a rich man, Rachel. Soon you'll see the house I had built. I think you'll like it."

83

He glanced at her. She sat ramrod straight, looking straight ahead.

"I hope you'll be happy here."

She nodded stiffly and spoke without emotion. "I'm sure we will. The country is beautiful." They topped a rise, and she gasped. "Is that your house?"

"That's *our* house if you'll marry me."

She faced him. "I am a woman of my word. You can trust me as well." She turned back and looked at the scene in front of them. "It's wonderful."

"I'm glad it pleases you. I see my foreman is already there with your children." Yes, the yard had never sported so many youngsters. He had to admit, his heart warmed at the sight of so many little ones frolicking in the yard. It's what he and Clara had dreamed about, but it had never happened. Not with her.

Rachel smiled. "I thought about what you said. I'll sew a patch with my children's names and pin it on them until you can remember who they are." She laughed. "Now that I think about it, meeting them all at once would be a daunting task."

He joined her laughter. "Good. Sounds like a workable plan. I'll study hard, so they don't have to wear them too long."

Her eyes brightened. "They are good children. All of them."

"I'll treat them as my own. My place has been quiet far too long." Almost to the house, he heard a string of Chinese in George's high-pitched voice. The judge said a quick prayer that the man didn't scare the kids.

Rachel let out a worried. "Oh my."

"That's George. He's my houseboy, cook, and friend. Been with me for ten years. He's not dangerous."

"Hurry, get me to my children."

The judge drove the carriage to the yard and stopped. Before he could get down, she'd jumped out of the buggy and was running for her children. But her anxiety was for nothing. George had a plate of cookies and a gaggle of kids around him. Yes, he could trust George with the new family.

He looped the reins over the post and went to the happy reunion. "George, I see you've met Rachel and her family."

George bowed. "Yes, Missy Dowd and childrens. Wonderful."

The judge grinned. "Now, maybe I should meet these children. We weren't formally introduced at the station."

Rachel smiled. "Yes. Children, get in order and tell Judge Solomon who you are and your age."

One little boy stepped out of line. "Like we practiced, Mama?"

"Yes, like we practiced."

He scurried to the boys' line and stood at the end next to his look alike.

Rachel came and stood alongside the judge. "All right children."

The first boy, man really, came in front of him and shook his hand. "William Dowd, I'm twenty."

The oldest girl came next. "Sarah, I'm eighteen and so happy for you and my mother."

Right behind her, a tall blonde boy stepped up to him. "James, sir and I am sixteen."

"Benjamin, Fourteen."

A smiling girl sauntered toward him. "Julia, I'm twelve. I like dolls."

Rachel cleared her throat. "Just your names and ages."

A shy red-headed girl with freckles stood in front of him, looked down, and mumbled. "Penelope. I'm ten. I like your horses."

She was almost pushed aside by a rambunctious girl. "Annie, and I'm eight."

"Kathleen, six." A young one lisped.

The two look-a-likes stepped forward together. "I'm Terrence." The shyer one looked down. "I'm Lawrence."

Rachel held out her arms and enveloped the twins in a hug. "Larry and Terry. They are a handful but have brought such joy to us all."

The judge nodded. "Welcome to the Rockin' C. We have the biggest ranch in Solomon's Valley. And yes, Penelope, we have horses. Once we get to know one another better, I'll have Matt, he's my foreman, pick out a horse fit for each of you." He faced Rachel. "If your mother approves that is."

Shouts of "can we mother" rang through the air.

Rachel smiled with her eyes. "Yes. That would be fine."

The gong announcing dinner chimed. "That is my, well the man who keeps the house and cooks for me. His name is George. And that gong was to let us know dinner is ready." The judge held his arm out toward the house. "We'll eat and then you can all pick out your rooms."

He hoped George had cooked something the children would like. At times, the ornery old Chinaman made dishes that he doubted even those in China would eat.

The judge walked up the porch and to the door. Pulling the big longhorn handle, he held it open for his family to enter. He had to admit that just thinking the word fired a warm spot in his heart. Then again, by the looks on some of the older kids faces, he had doubts and hoped he'd not have a feud in his own home. They'd not take to their mother with a new husband easily. Would be hard for anyone.

Rachel waited by his side. "Thank you, again. I believe this will be a good arrangement. I hope you aren't too angry about my hiding the number of children I have."

The judge shook his head. "My ranch and house are big enough for them all." He studied her.

Arrangement. That is what they'd settled on. A marriage of companionship. He'd provide for her and her children, and she'd be at his side to keep him from being lonely.

Rachel entered and rushed to the twins who were *admiring* a bronze figure of a horse.

The judge wondered if they would ever be a real family.

Chapter 9

When Rachel had first seen the big two-story house rising up from the grasslands, her worries that she and her children would overwhelm whatever arrangements Sol might have had evaporated. When Sol had said they could all pick out their rooms, he had meant it.

A twinge of fear pricked her heart. Did that include a room for her? She had said in the letters that she would perform her wifely duties. Yet now, she was terrified. She'd had no such qualms with her husband, but they'd been in love, not merely, well for lack of a better word, partners.

Sol gently touched her elbow and ushered her toward the dining room. The house was rugged much like the man beside her. Yet, surprisingly clean with the smell of wood, books, and the most delicious aroma of fried chicken.

She rescued a sculpture of a horse from the twins. "Children, keep your hands to yourselves."

Sol nodded at her. "We'll set some rules down later, but I don't want the children to think they're living in a museum."

Rachel felt as if she'd walked into a fairy tale. This was all too good to be true. She glanced at Sol. Why had he remained alone for so long? Why did he have to resort to a mail order bride?

"I thought we'd sit together at the end of the table." Sol pulled a chair out for her.

The table was long and built of rugged polished wood. The chairs were also built of thick wood for rugged men of the west. The dishes weren't fancy. In fact, nothing in the house, so far, had a woman's touch. She tried to remember when Sol had said his wife had died.

George served the food. He was such a small man but a huge delight. He sat at the end next to the twins and helped them with their plates. It touched her mother's heart to see the way the older man took to Larry. Her little son had taken her husband's death the hardest. Much harder than his twin.

Kathleen dug her fork into the potatoes.

Rachel stopped her. "Children, we always give thanks."

Sol cleared his throat. "Sorry, guess I better do that right now because I know how hard it is to wait when you're hungry and have George's food in front of you."

Actually, he wondered why the Chinaman had never made him fried chicken before.

He bowed his head. "Father, I thank you for this food. More than that, I thank you for sending this family to me. To the Rockin' C. Bless each one of them and help them to feel at home in this place. Amen."

The children shouted "Amen" and followed it up with forks scraping on plates. Embarrassed for her rowdy brood, Rachel glanced at the judge and started to apologize.

He sat back in his chair, enjoying a chicken leg, but the look on his face set her at ease. He didn't look like a man who'd just been overwhelmed by a large clan. No, he had the proud look of a man surveying his family.

Rachel turned to her food and enjoyed the dinner. Perhaps this would work out. Perhaps even she could be happy again.

After dinner, Sol rose. "There's at least an hour of sunlight left. Why don't you children run off some steam and explore the yard? There's a litter of pups in the barn. Matt will show them to you if you ask him. Your mother and I have things to discuss."

William, brows furrowed and ever the watchful one, glanced at her.

She smiled to put him at ease. "William, will you and the older ones watch out for the younger? I will be fine."

He started to protest.

"William, I am fine."

"Yes, ma'am." He scooped up the twins, one in each arm. "Let's go. I know a couple of little boys who would like to see those pups."

She turned to Sol. "He's a good son. I fear I leaned on him a bit too much after my husband's death." Rachel wanted to go on and talk and avoid whatever it was the judge wanted to discuss with her.

"Rachel, I know this can't be easy for you. I wanted to let you know that I have a room picked out for you. It adjoins mine." He put up a hand and hurriedly added, "There's a lock on the door that you'll control. And like I said, until we're married, I'll sleep in the bunkhouse."

Tears stung her eyes. Could he be this good? "Thank you for your thoughtfulness." She wanted to break down and cry. Had this man thought of everything? Then her glee froze. Surely, he had. What would the night bring?

^^^

The judge held his hand out to her. "Would you like to see your room?"

Like a timid bird, she rose and placed her shaking hand in his. "Yes."

He wanted to kick himself. What was he thinking? She'd obviously gotten the wrong idea. "Perhaps a tour of the house first?"

She nodded with thankfulness in her eyes.

He led her to his study. "My office with all my law books. I spend a lot of time in here. It's become my favorite place." He stopped and let her explore the shelves.

She ran her gloved hand over the volumes. "You have a good selection of books. I'm glad to see that. I would like it if my children could read these. Books were scarce in Minnesota."

"I'd be delighted to share them with the children. We can order more. It's a good way to see the world."

With a glow in her eyes, she gave him a slight smile. "I'd love that."

"George has always done the cooking, but if you want to, the kitchen is yours. He understands that."

Throwing him a harried gaze, she nodded. "Thank you. I do want my children to continue to enjoy some of their favorite dishes. Swedish meatballs, Kroppkakor, a kind of filled potato dumpling. Cinnamon buns. Other things they enjoy."

He grinned. "Sounds good to me. Clara was Hungarian and had dishes from the old country that we enjoyed."

"Clara?"

His face grew hot. "My wife. She died eight years ago. The fever took her and then our daughter Shirley."

Sadness swallowed the joy in her eyes. "Oh. I am sorry. Death is such an avid hunter. My Frank died and long before, it also claimed our first son, Franklin Jr."

Hating that they had such sadness in common, he took her hand. "Let's see the kitchen. If there is anything missing, tell me, and we can order it."

"Thank you, Sol. You're a kind man."

He stared into her eyes. They were green with a touch of blue or maybe gray and reminded him of Sapphire Lake in the summer. He wondered if her statement was one of belief or hope. He sensed she was wary of what would become of her in the night, he decided to avoid the upstairs until the children came in and they all picked out their rooms.

He proudly showed her the parlor. She liked all the furniture that Clara had agonized over in choosing. It was the one room that had retained his wife's feminine touch. Finished with the grand tour of the bottom floor, he stopped at the front door.

"I thought we should let the children pick out their rooms while it's still light."

Relief showed on her face. "Yes. Thank you."

He opened the door and grinned. "I guess the puppies are making a grand impression."

She laughed. "Yes, I think you're right. We had to leave our old dog at home on the farm. Oh, don't worry. He'll be well taken care of. The new owners promised me that."

Sol put a hand on the small of her back. "Shall we go see the pups?"

She didn't answer but trotted down the steps.

He watched her run toward her children. They were family. Would he ever be a part of it? He hoped so. Sent a prayer to the Lord and asked for wisdom befitting his name. He would need it. As he approached the children and the pups, he noticed William's wary gaze.

The boy was worried about his mother. Sol didn't blame him. William was a grown man. He'd have to talk with him and find out what plans he had for his life. There was plenty of work on the ranch, but if William wanted college, he'd see to it that the boy had every opportunity.

Rachel picked up a plump little female pup. "Oh, they are so cute." She turned and begged him with longing in her eyes. "This one. She reminds me of a dog I had when I was a little girl."

Sol walked over to her and patted the silky pup. "You want her? She's yours."

Tears moistened her eyes. "Could I keep her in the house? In my room?"

He nodded. "She's likely to keep you awake for a few nights."

One of the little girls ran to him and wrapped her arms around his legs. "Can I have one for my room?"

Sol knelt to face her. "I don't have enough pups for everyone to have one."

She frowned and counted to six. "Nope, I guess you don't. But there's enough for me to have one."

Rachel gasped. "Annie. That's enough."

Sol laughed. "Tell you what. Why don't the girls pick one out and the boys pick one out? Then you can all share the puppies."

One of the boys grabbed a rambunctious black and white puppy. "What kind are they?"

"They're sheepdogs. Their parents came from Wales."

"Wale dogs. Sounds kind of strange to me."

Rachel laughed. "Benjamin, he said they are sheepdogs from Wales, a country near England."

Penelope counted again. "That leaves three left. Who is going to take them?"

Sol smiled at her. "Just so happens, I have three of them sold. In fact, their new owners are coming to get them next week."

The children sighed.

William put down the pup he'd picked up. "We can't afford to pay for a dog."

Sol faced him. "What's mine is yours, son."

William's green eyes flashed. "I'm not your son." He turned and ran out of the barn.

Rachel shot him a pained look before turning to run after him.

Sol caught her arm. "Let him go. He needs time to figure things out."

She turned to him. "I'm sorry. I guess I—"

"No, it's all right. If he didn't have some fire in him, I'd be worried. Let me and William work things out between us."

She nodded and held her pup close. "Thank you for the dogs."

"My pleasure, Rachel. Truly my pleasure." He clapped his hands to get the children's' attention. "Let's go pick out your rooms."

Like a small herd, the children scampered excitedly for the house. Sol had to grin. Seems his quiet days and nights were a thing of the past. He glanced at Rachel. "I'll let you and the kids choose their rooms. I'll get my things and set up camp in the bunkhouse."

"Thank you, Sol. You have been most kind to me and the children." Her eyes caught the setting sun and gleamed with a bright green.

He could get used to having her around. "I'm leaving early tomorrow morning. I have business to attend to. I hope you'll make yourself at home."

She frowned slightly. "You will be gone long?"

"No. Most of the morning. Then I'll have to see how things go. I've got to solve that feud problem I was telling you about. I have a lot of praying to do tonight and tomorrow. I'll need the wisdom of Solomon."

She laughed. "I believe you'll come up with just the right solution. My children and I will manage."

He left her at the bottom of the stairs and started for his study.

"Sol, thank you." She hugged the pup in her arms.

"I'm glad you're here, Rachel." Not wanting the awkward silence to return, he left her for the seclusion of his study.

Chapter 10

The judge threw off the blanket. He'd struggled most the night with how to handle the feud, but answers had evaded him as deftly as sleep. Being as quiet as possible, he dressed and was almost out the bunkhouse door when Matt called out to him.

"It's still dark outside." In minutes, Matt was at his side.

Thankful for his foreman, the judge pointed at the door. "Care to go on a night ride with me? I could use the company."

"Yes, sir." Matt grabbed his pants and shirt. "Give me a minute, and I'll saddle the horses. Big Sandy?"

"No. This is likely to be a wild day. Might as well start it with the black. And, Matt, I can saddle my own horse."

"Yes, sir." He stepped into his boots and slapped his hat on his mussed hair.

On the walk to the barn, the judge tried not to worry about the decision he needed to make. Sure, he could involve the council, but he knew what they'd say. "Kick them out of the valley." That decision would likely result in bloodshed.

The black snorted at being wakened so early. After saddling the skittish horse, the judge mounted the animal and questioned his choice as the horse coiled like a rattler ready for a strike. It was going to be a hard ride. So much for having time to think, then again, maybe that's what he needed to take his mind off the problem.

The easiest thing to do would be to have one or both of the families leave the valley. Buy them out. Run them off their land. Their homes. No, he couldn't do that. Both families had been here the same amount of time. After talking with them, he knew neither had family elsewhere. He was trying to stop a war not start it.

The black shied as a gust of wind blew leaves across the trail. The judge held the reins tight and circled the big stallion to regain control. "Ah, you bronc. You're not helping me."

Matt rode alongside him and patted his mustang. "My dun and your black get along. I'll ride close, might help settle your wild horse down some."

"Thanks, Matt. Sorry I've not been talkative." He glanced at the dun gelding and noticed his black was calming down.

An idea nagged at him. Could he be that bold to suggest such a thing? Might work. The judge grinned. "Let's get to town."

Matt grinned. "You look like a man with an idea."

"Might have one. When we get to town, round up the town council, and have them meet me at the courthouse."

"Will do. There's enough light now, and the road is even. How about we let these horses run some of the wild out of them?"

"Matt, that's an excellent idea." The judge tapped the sides of his horse and let the stallion gallop. Riding a horse at a run was the closest thing to flying. Freedom. With a grin, he reckoned how he wasn't too old to enjoy the thrill. No, he wasn't old at all. He'd come up with a plan to solve the feud. A woman and her family lived in his house. Yes, life was becoming good again. *Forgive me, Clara. For the first time in those eight long years since you left me, I feel alive.*

The sun winked over the hill proclaiming the new day just as the judge rode into town. He nodded at Matt and left him to go to the courthouse. The judge opened the door and relaxed. This was his home. Where he felt at ease. He breathed in the smell of books and pipe tobacco. His courthouse. Territory law, miner's law, and the law of the west. The law was his first love.

He stopped. Love. Was it right to think of your profession as your first love when you just invited a woman to be your wife? A warm, beautiful woman at that. Surprised, the judge pictured Rachel with her dark, cinnamon-colored hair and not Clara's blond.

Yet, Rachel hadn't come out here for love. She came for security. He'd promised her that.

Footsteps signaled the council had arrived.

Putting thoughts of Rachel aside, he sat behind his desk, breathed in the smell of the law books, and thought how at home he felt.

Matt opened the door and ushered in the council. Mr. Satchel, Earl Hollander, the owner of the mercantile. Jed Chandler, the assayer and land man. Lee Calhoun owner of the feed store. And Jake Deeds, the undertaker. Dolly Preston owner of the dress shop, and Fallon, owner of the Gilded Lady Saloon.

The judge stood. "Thank you all for coming. I've come up with a solution for the Murphy-Howard feud. But I need all of you to cooperate with my decision. It won't work if you all don't go along."

"Count me in, Judge." Earl Hollander stepped forward. "Whatever you decide, if those two families don't go along with it, I'll deny them supplies."

"Thanks, Earl. That's exactly what I need all of you to do." He eyed the men and woman and knew he had their agreement.

Fallon rubbed the butt of the always-present pistol attached to his hip. "We're all tired of their fighting. Not good for business. Not even my business." He grinned. "I'm curious as to what you've decided."

The others murmured their agreement and curiosity.

Holding up his hands to quiet the crowd, the judge nodded. "I'll tell you the same time as I tell the families."

Matt opened the door and let another enter.

To the judge's surprise, William entered and then held the door so Rachel could come inside.

She sought his eyes and smiled. "I hope it's all right if I sit in on your decision."

The crowd parted as she made her way to his desk.

He came around to her side. "Everyone, this is Rachel Dowd and her son, William. She's agreed to be my bride."

Cheers echoed in the room.

"And yes, I'm delighted that you've come to hear my decision and what I hope will be the end to this feud. Sorry I don't have enough chairs for everyone to take a seat. But if you all will stand along the wall. I'll need your votes when the time comes to persuade the Murphys and Howards that it'd be wise for them to agree to the terms."

He walked Rachel around the desk and seated her to the side. Her presence gave him confidence. He hoped she'd agree with his decision.

Loud shouts and grumbles signaled the arriving families. Their anger and hatred still intact despite burying Anna and Stephen made the judge more determined to make his idea work.

"Come in, Murphys to the left, Howards to the right." He waited for the families to find their places.

"Ben Murphy, Nina Howard, please step forward."

The two did.

"The town of Shirleyville has made a decision regarding your families. We are all tired of having to divide to accommodate your hatred for one another. It ends today."

Ben sneered. "It's not going to be that easy."

Nina shook her head.

"No, Ben. I don't think it will be easy. For your families that is. For the rest of us, we've made up our minds." He gestured to the council.

"From this day, Ben Murphy, your oldest son will no longer live with you. Daniel will live with the Howards and help take care of them. As a family of females, the Howards need a man around to protect them and care for their ranch."

Ronan shouted. "No!" And charged forward.

Ben grabbed his son. "How dare you. It's not right. You can't."

The judge banged his gavel. "I'm not through. Nina Howard. From this day forward, Aileen will live with the Murphys. She will be treated as one of their family. Loved and protected as if she were their own. A home without a woman's touch is not a home." The judge nearly choked on the reality of that statement. He'd learned that after eight long years.

Nina grabbed her oldest daughter. "What kind of law is that? You have no right—"

The judge glared at her and then Ben. "This town has every right. We have put up with your nonsense far too long. You will either abide by the rules or leave the valley. You have until Saturday to comply. I'll be by the Murphys to make sure they've built a room suitable for Aileen. Daniel, you can sleep in the barn until you build yourself a room at the Howards. And I better hear that each of the new additions to your families is being treated with the utmost respect and civility."

Aileen glanced at Daniel and then sobbed in her mother's arms.

Seeing the pain in her eyes, the judge prayed he'd made the right decision. However, he just didn't see any other way to help those two families get over their hatred for one another.

He banged his gavel. "The decree is approved." He glanced at Nina. "You can visit one another."

"How long is this to go on?"

Ben stepped up beside her. "Yeah. How long am I going to have to have a Howard in my home?"

The judge glared at him. "Until you can talk about the Howards in a civil tone. Until you can tell me you love Aileen as if she was your daughter and you don't want to see her leave."

"You're crazy, Judge." Ben grabbed Ronan just as he burst forward with fist raised.

Mr. Satchel came forward. "All of us on the town council agree with the decision. We won't sell or do business with you or the Howards if you don't go through with the judgment. You two families have made us all suffer because of your crazy feud. We're done with it."

"I'll have my foreman deliver materials and oversee building Aileen's room." The judge darted a look to Rachel.

He relaxed. Her admiration for his decision was clear in the smile she gave him. She stood, and he went to her side.

Rachel gently touched his arm. "The wisdom of Solomon. You split two households to save them. Hope it works. I have to say, I don't pity that girl going to a strange house with all those men."

He stared into her eyes. Was she talking about herself? Fear of being in a strange house with him. A man she doesn't know. His heart went out to her. Why had he never considered how hard it would be for a woman to leave her home and go to a faraway land and live in a house that wasn't her own?

People began filing out of the courthouse. He waited and walked her to the door. "You know I was

109

thinking if there's anything you want to buy for the house, something that would make it feel more like your home, feel free to get it. Just tell them to put it on my bill."

Tears moistened her eyes. She nodded and glanced at William and then back. "Thank you, Sol. Perhaps William and I will look around and meet you at home."

Even though she hesitated before saying the word, Sol's heart warmed that she'd said it. He wanted her to think of the big house as her home. Her children, too. William, well he was a question mark. The boy looked surprised at the mention of his mother buying something. Yet, his wary expression soon returned.

Rachel cleared her throat. "Sol, I would like to order some roses to put around the house. Would that be agreeable to you?"

He patted her hand. "Yes. You're not to worry about expenses. Order whatever you want."

She pulled her hand from his but smiled. "Thank you. William and I will meet you later."

"All right, I should be leaving in a couple of hours. I'll have Matt accompany you. There are dangerous men who roam these parts. I'd feel better if you and William didn't ride out alone."

William took his mother's arm. "I can take care of her. Of all of us."

"Now, son. I didn't mean to infer you couldn't. I just want to be sure you're safe. This land—"

"I'm not your son. I brought my rifle, and I know how to use it."

Not wanting to make a scene, the judge nodded. "Didn't mean to get you riled. I'll see you both at home." He left the courthouse without looking back. Rachel's oldest had gotten under his skin. Yes, he could understand why the boy was upset. But he'd not abide rude behavior by anyone. He'd have to speak to Rachel about that.

He waved down Matt. "You have the wood for the girl's room at the Murphy's?"

"Yes, sir. We were just about to ride over there and get things started. Think the families will go for your decision?"

"I think so. The alternative is they move out. Neither one looks like they're ready to do that."

Matt tapped a finger on the wood post outside the courthouse. "The girl's mother looks pretty tore up about the decision."

The judge gathered his horse's reins. "That she does. I'm hoping the families will come to their senses. I'm not holding my breath, though. Not with those two."

"No, sir. I'm not either."

The judge mounted, checked to see if he could find Rachel and spotted her just as she was entering the mercantile. William was behind her, tipping his hat to Bridgett. The judge hauled in a deep breath. That looked like more trouble. That girl had half the men in the valley wrapped around her little finger. He'd have to speak to Rachel about that, too.

The ride to the Murphy's was quiet on his part. Not on Ben's part. He filled every silent gap with angry words about how unfair the decision was. The judge was about to regret not running the families out of the valley when Daniel rode in between them.

"Judge, I want you to know, I think your decision was a wise one. Not saying I like it, but wise nonetheless. I'll miss my brothers, but those women do need some help. Even when Mr. Howard was alive, things went to disrepair. I'll protect them as if they were my own family and work hard to clean the place up." Daniel faced the judge. "But I won't work the sheep. I'm a cattleman."

The judge smiled. "All right, Daniel. You protect the girls. Hunt for food for them and fix up the place. They can handle the sheep. I'm giving them one of my sheepdogs to go with the one they already have and it should help them round up the curly critters."

"I don't see how you can allow the stinking animals on cattle land."

"I figured it was what a family of girls could raise." He eyed the boy. "Not going to have any trouble out of you, am I?"

"No. No trouble. When can I visit my family?"

"I figure Sundays would be a good day for you and Aileen to go back to your families. I figure Ronan or one of your brothers can escort her home, stay for supper, and then see her back."

Ben growled. "You just got us all figured to play nice with one another. I'll abide by your decision, but I won't like it. I'll be kind to the girl, but she's a Howard and nothing is going to change that."

The judge caught a light spark in Daniel's eye and grinned to himself. "Maybe, Ben. Things can change and that's what I'm counting on. I would think about now, you and your boys might enjoy female cooking. I hear Aileen is a serious cook and has learned well from her mother."

A grunt was the only answer.

The judge grinned to himself. His plan was perfect. He hoped so anyway. It was time the valley had some peace. They still had the outlaws to deal with, but the town wouldn't have to divide because of the feud.

Then there was Rachel and her children. How would they fit into his life? Would they let him fit into theirs? That oldest boy, William, didn't exactly look agreeable to the marriage. The judge shook his head. "Things were sure easier when you were here, Clara."

Chapter 11

Rachel flipped through the pages of the catalog and pointed out the Bouquet dOr, a yellow climber, and a tea rose that was a pink. She would add more if they survived the Montana winters. She sighed, just the idea of having the fragrance made her homesick. Her roses had been her salvation on the farm.

Frank had chided her on more than one occasion that he ought to quit farming crops and raise flowers. She sighed at the remembrance of him, and the good times they'd had together. An image of Sol slipped into her mind. Would they be able to put away the past and enjoy one another? Or would they merely be companions brought together because of need?

Her cheeks flushed warmly. She prayed that *need* would be held at bay for some time. She wasn't ready to consider her wifely duties just yet.

William tapped her shoulder, causing her to jump.

"Mother, are you ready to go? I think we should leave so we aren't out at dark."

"Yes." She thanked the storeowner, embarrassed that she had forgotten his name. She wasn't the best at remembering people's names. She laughed to herself, perhaps she used up all her naming faculties with her brood. "Let's get home. I miss the children."

He laughed. "I'm sure they're fine. They were excited to play with the pups today." He grew quiet, his face taking on a pensive expression. After she was seated in the wagon, he climbed in beside her.

"Mother, are you sure you want to marry the judge?"

Rachel stilled her racing doubts. She mustn't let him see her indecision and fear. "William, it is why we are here. I trust the judge is a good man. He's treated us with nothing but kindness."

"I don't like it. I could get a job. I could—"

"William, you are a good son, but you are not my husband or responsible for providing for the family. You have your own life to live. Have you thought any more about Sue Goodfert? I thought you and she had talked about marriage."

He shook his head. "No. We weren't right for one another. Once Father died, she drifted away from me. She wants a man who can provide a good and easy life for her."

"I see." Rachel began to understand some of her son's discomfort at the arrangement between her and

116

Sol. "William, don't judge me too harshly for the decision I have made to marry Sol. He is a good man. He will provide nicely for me and all of you children. Give him a chance."

Her son's jaw muscles tightened, but he held his tongue and remained silent. She could feel his displeasure. That angered her. Life for a woman alone wasn't easy or full of opportunities, especially when she had ten children to care for. She was fortunate to have found Sol and that he had agreed to take on her children.

She rubbed William's arm. "We will have good times again. Sol is a good man. I can feel that in my heart. He will be a good father to the younger ones. Perhaps a good mentor to the older ones and you."

"I don't want anything to do with him. He will never be my father."

"I understand, but please don't come between his relationship with the younger ones. Or me."

William shot a quick glance her way. After a few moments of strained silence, he shrugged. "All right. If that's what you want."

"It is. I want your brothers and sisters to have this chance at a good life. You too."

117

"I don't need him in my life. I'll stay until I'm sure you and the kids are safe, and then I'll take off on my own. I can make my own way in the world."

Tears pricked her eyes. Proud and capable. He was so much like his father. "You will do fine, William. Just promise me one thing." She took the reins and pulled the horse to a halt.

William turned to face her, sadness in his eyes.

"I want you to give Sol a chance. Open your eyes to the possibility that he is a good man. Listen to him and trust my decision to marry him."

"Do you love him? I mean, you can't possibly. You've only known him for a day." He shifted in the seat. "How can you forget Father so easily?"

"Oh, William. I will never forget your father, but he is no longer with us. Life must go on for the living. The children need more than I can give them. They need the love of a good man. A father. You had that. The younger ones can barely remember their father."

William lowered his head and nodded. "All right, Mother. I'll give it a chance. I'll stay on until summer."

"Good." She looked about them and fell in love with the country. "Just look at the land, William. The lush grass. Breathtaking mountains in the distance.

Clear streams. This land is full of possibilities. And Sol. He's a good man. Look how the Lord provided a home big enough for us all. I feared we'd all be crammed in a small cabin. Ah, William. The Lord has provided us with a grand chance. Let's keep our minds on the goodness of God and the provision He has granted us."

"Get up, horses." William didn't answer, didn't look around at the beauty, and flinched at her mention of God.

Rachel's heart moaned for her son. That he felt let down by his father for dying and God for allowing it was all too evident. She'd seen the storm brewing. It was but a matter of time before William exploded. She prayed that Sol was an understanding man.

^^^

The judge watched as wood was unloaded and his men set to work building Aileen's room. He had to admit, looking at the mess at the Murphy's gave him doubts as to his decision. Well, he'd have to check on her regularly.

He pointed to the yard. "Ronan, you and Adam pick up the yard here. Make the place presentable for Aileen. I want her to cook and clean for you all, but she's not to be your slave. I'll be checking on her. Ben, I expect Aileen to be treated special. Understand?"

Ben growled. "Women are to clean and take care of the house. Said I was to treat her as my daughter."

Anger soured the judge's mood. "I want you to treat her as if she were *my* daughter. I better hear she's happy."

"Happy! You taking her away from her family and my boy from his and you expect them or us to be happy? No, we'll not be happy. I don't expect Daniel will, and I know this lass coming to stay here won't be. I'll see she is treated with respect. See that she has all the comfort I can afford her. But she's still a Howard, and we're still Murphys. You're wrong on this one judge."

"Maybe. But it's this way, or I kick both of your families from the valley. The town and I can't put up with your silly feud any longer."

Ben's eyes flamed. "You went way out of your jurisdiction on this one. You know nothing of what went on. The reason for the hatred between us. This crazy idea of yours won't work. There is nothing that will make me tolerate a Howard. Nothing."

"We'll see. For now, I better not see or hear of Aileen being mistreated by you or your sons. Clear?"

A nod was the only answer he got.

The room was well on its way to completion when the judge mounted his horse to leave for home. He left instructions with Matt and his men to stay until the building was finished and the ranch tidied up. He didn't want the girl coming to a complete mess.

After a last warning to Ben and his sons, the judge turned toward his home. To Rachel. To his new family.

Did Rachel find his house to her liking? Did she like him? Would she? A mourning dove cooed in a nearby tree. The eerie sound struck a familiar chord in his heart. Clara had loved the sound the birds made.

"Clara. You're going to have to step aside and give Rachel some room." As he finished saying the words, he heard in his heart, as if Clara were saying, "I've moved on, you must, too."

The words stung him. She'd left him. Not purposefully. But she'd left him all the same. Left him alone. For eight lonely years, he'd struggled to hold onto her. Dreamed of her. Pictured her in the flowery meadow she'd loved so. Ate her favorite meals, alone. She had moved on.

What is it the preacher had said, "She's passed over to paradise. To the mansion the Lord made for her. You can go to her later when your days are up, but for now, you need to live your life here. Without Clara."

The dove cooed its mournful call again. This time, the judge drank in the sound and remembered how it had made Clara smile. "All right, Clara. Yes, the sound is peaceful. I'm moving on now. Hope you'll be pleased, but even if you aren't, I have to live my life here in this world."

He clicked to the stallion and set him in a lope toward home. To a woman who'd come to live with him. To Rachel.

Chapter 12

Rachel shuddered to think how quickly the week had gone by. Sunday, she was to marry Sol. At their home. Her choice. She hadn't wanted a big show to the neighbors or town. However, to her chagrin, they were coming to the judge's house. Her house.

They'd really had little time alone together. Not a hard thing to understand with ten children, two puppies, and a half-crazy Chinaman under foot. Not to mention the foreman and hands that happened by to get orders or look inquisitively at the judge's new family.

The children had settled down for the most part. The younger ones were enamored of Sol. Her four oldest, a little more reserved down to William's outright disdain for her future husband. Sarah was pleased and happy. She thought Sol would be a good husband.

"Besides, Mama, he's a handsome man. Doesn't look old at all. You make a splendid couple."

Rachel pulled in a sigh to quiet her thoughts. William was near, and she didn't want him worrying about her which invariably would lead to a *discussion* on why she shouldn't marry. She thought Sol was handsome. She'd even had schoolgirl tingles when she sat near him. When he touched her arm or hand. When she thought of being alone with him.

What he thought, she had no idea. He kept his feelings locked inside the vault to his heart. He was cordial, kind, and thoughtful to her and her family. Even William. But they had not sat down and talked as couples should. As she and Frank had done many times.

So, tomorrow was the big day. The night she dreaded. Had he worn out his patience? He didn't show it. Perhaps they could get alone together today and talk. She wanted, needed, some idea of how he felt about her. What he expected from her. What he would demand of her on her wedding night.

And in the house with her ten children and the Chinaman, all those ears and questions, made her anxious. The twins still ran into her room early mornings to sleep with her. She couldn't bear the thought of them finding Sol in her bed, too.

William. What was she to do with him? He practically dared her to not care for Sol as if it were a personal affront to Frank's memory.

To avoid the panic that was stalking her, she pushed the thoughts from her mind. "Monday, it will be over."

Sol happened to walk by at that moment and stopped. "What?"

Startled at his presence and attention, she darted a quick glance to William and then to Sol. "Oh, nothing."

He held his hat and twisted it around. A habit he had whenever he needed to tell her something. "I was wondering if you'd go with me when I take Aileen to the Murphys'? Today is the big day of the switch."

"Oh, yes. Let me get my shawl." She avoided William's dark glare and bolted for her room. The poor girl. To be singled out to live in a house full of men. Rude, dirty men at that. She'd thought Sol's decision brilliant until she put herself in Aileen's shoes. Heavens, Rachel felt estranged enough in Sol's house, and she wasn't a mere girl in a house full of strangers and worse, men who hated her family.

She practically ran down the stairs. Perhaps, this would be a time she could find out how Sol was feeling about her. "Ready."

"You look lovely."

Her cheeks flushed warmly. "Thank you." She called out to her oldest. "William, you and Sarah watch the children."

The boy didn't answer, just shrugged while glaring at Sol.

Outside, the wagon was hitched. Matt had everything they needed ready. He was truly Sol's right-hand man. She'd noticed he glared at William much like her son glared at Sol. He'd warrant watching. Rachel didn't want anyone threatening her children no matter their age.

Sol came to her side and helped her climb into the wagon. "It's a fine day for a ride in the country. I'm sorry it's going to take us most of the day. Hope you don't mind."

She smiled coyly. "No, I don't mind. George is a capable cook and housekeeper. He leaves me with little to do."

Sol patted her hand. "You have the children to tend to." He slapped the reins and urged the horses onward.

"Ah, he even helps with them. The twins adore him."

"From what I've seen of George and the twins, it's mutual."

She looked straight ahead, afraid to ask him the question she'd rehearsed all night. "I don't think we know one another adequately. For a marriage. Tomorrow."

"Oh?" Hurt and confusion rippled in his voice.

Her heart thumped so hard she feared he could hear it. "I was wondering if you wouldn't mind if we postponed it for a time. I think we both have memories of what we had before. I just need some more time."

She stared at the side of his face, for he had turned from her. He was a young looking forty. She prayed she looked the match for him. There were days she felt old, used up, and dead inside.

Disappointment darkened his eyes. "I see. If that's what you want, I can wait."

Had he changed his mind? Not that she wouldn't blame him. After all, he'd left his own house and was sleeping in the bunkhouse. His home turned over to a woman and ten children. Overrun being the proper word.

He stopped the wagon and turned to face her. "Rachel, I want us to have a chance at real happiness together."

"What if we don't, can't—"

"I have no doubts. From the moment I first saw you at the stage depot, I felt we were meant to be together. I hope you're not disappointed."

She stared into his eyes. Dark blue like a summer sky. Yet, warm and accepting. His face lined from sunshine and wisdom. "I am not disappointed, but we don't know one another very well. I have no idea how you feel about me or the children. We have hardly been alone together." She drew in a breath. Not that she wanted to be alone with him. Not at night. Not yet, anyway.

"I agree. So, today we'll have some time. Do you have any questions for me?" He slapped the reins gently and moved the horses on.

"I'm not sure. I didn't want to have a session of cross-examination as if I were a witness in your court. I merely want to get to know you the way couples do."

He nodded. "All right. We'll make sure we take time together. For starters, you can accompany me when I check on Aileen and Daniel. It's a nice ride, you'll see. Today we have to take the wagon to carry Aileen's things to the Murphys, but other times we can ride horses. You do ride, don't you?"

She shrugged. "I was a farmer's wife. We had horses, but not for riding. They were for pulling the plow and wagon."

"I'll teach you. Matt's working on a mare that will be perfect for you. That is if you want to learn." He gazed at her with an eager look on his face as if he hoped she would want to ride.

She'd never had the desire. In fact, she found horses to be a bit scary. So large and with stories of friends and family hurt by them. Yet, somehow, she sensed this was important to him. "I guess I could learn. You will need to be patient with me, though."

He laughed. "I'll do that. When you feel ready. If you'd like, you can order some riding clothes or material if you want to make your own. Some of the ladies out west use a split skirt. I can order a sidesaddle for you. Or you can learn on a western saddle."

"I really have no idea what is expected, preferred, or respectable."

"Rachel, this is the west. What's more, we live in my valley. Solomon's Valley. When we go to the Howards, I'll introduce you to Cassidy. She's a young woman who rides better than most men. She's a little wild, but she can tell you all about riding as a woman."

129

"At home," she paused. "Sorry, in Minnesota, I worked the farm. Planted the garden. I would like to have a garden. I don't know what vegetables grow in these parts, but I enjoyed working with the dirt and making sure my family had food stored for the winter. And flowers. I love flowers."

"I want you to be happy. A garden you shall have. Order whatever plants you want. I'll have the men plow up a section for you." He glanced at her inquisitively. "You do know that I have a lot of money. We don't have to work hard. Do you want to travel?"

A giddy shiver traveled through Rachel's veins. She'd never in all her life lived in abundance. Not of money. Oh, she and Frank had had good years, but with ten children to provide for, there just had never been any extra money.

She tampered down the smile that wanted to take over her face. "I'll have to think about that Sol. I'm afraid you didn't order a woman of means to be your bride. I hope I don't disappoint you."

"Nonsense. I believe the Lord arranged to send me the woman I needed. I prayed before I sent that letter to the agency." He kept his gaze ahead.

How could he be so sure? She wasn't. Not at all. She'd not had the luxury of choosing a man. Sol had been the only one to respond to her ad with the agency. She was sure he could have chosen any woman, even a younger one who would give him his own children.

"Sol, why me? You could have had your pick." She stared at the side of his head, wishing he would turn to face her so she could see the truth of his words in his eyes.

He drew in a breath and faced her. "There was something in your letter that tugged at me. Pulled at my soul. After I read it, there could be no one else. I can't explain it. Perhaps it was the working of the Lord on my heart, but whatever the reason or cause, I believed you were the woman for me."

She tested his words. His eyes proclaimed them as truth. He truly wanted her. Rachel Dowd, a used-up farmer's wife. What did she think? The truth. She didn't trust him. Why would he want her? She was nothing special. Not rich. Not a lady of means. Certainly not beautiful.

His eyes continued to bore into her as if peeling away the layers of the wall she'd erected around her heart. Even things she'd hidden from Frank. Things no one knew. Travel? How had Sol hit on the one thing she'd dreamed about since a small child. To see Europe where kings conquered lands. To see fine cities and museums. How could he have guessed her dream?

He urged the horses on. "And you? Why did you choose me?"

She hesitated. How could she tell him that she had no choice? He was the only one. Her only hope to keep her family together. The only man who showed an interest in her besides Harley McCreedy, a neighbor who had told her he'd take her on and the older boys to help out at his farm as more slave than heir.

"Sol, I must be honest. You were the only one who wanted me. And my children. And I didn't even tell you the truth about them. You could have sent me back."

He laughed. "I thought we had an orphan group come through. Then I saw them all around you. The Lord blessed me with abundance. Guess He figured I could handle ten children and a new wife."

She chuckled with him at what had to be a shock to him as he witnessed all her children coming from the coach. Then her thoughts turned somber. "You still can. Send me back. I wasn't honest with you about the children. I was so desperate to keep them with me. Keep my family together."

Sol stopped the wagon. He turned to her and took her hands in his. "Rachel, I will never turn you away. I meant what I said in the letter and just a few minutes ago. I've pledged my life and all I have to you and your children. I can't explain it, but it's almost a need inside me. To know that you'll be taken care of. That all that I've worked for will go to someone I love."

Her face grew warm. She hated it but knew she was blushing and near tears. How could he have such deep feelings for her already? "I hope I can love you as deeply. In time. I don't want to disappoint you."

He grinned. "You won't. I've got enough faith for the both of us right now. When you're ready, you tell me, and we'll have that wedding. Rachel, you never have to worry. I'll never turn you out."

"That is going to take me some time to understand. I can't help but feel you're getting the short end of the deal. I have nothing to offer you."

He looked down and then into her eyes. "Love. A family. Warmth on a cold night. Companionship as we watch the sun set. Someone to share the goodness and hardship of life. I've had my fill of loneliness. Eight

133

long years of it. I'm ready to share my life with another woman. You, Rachel, are the woman I want to grow old with." He chuckled. "Or perhaps make that older."

She shook her head. "You'll have to give me time to take it all in, Sol. I am just having a hard time understanding why you would want me. Thank you for being patient." Rachel wanted to believe the man sitting next to her. Wanted to, but didn't. Was he hiding some deep dark secret? Was he truly a good man? Why hadn't he married someone from around here sooner?

He slapped the reins and grinned. "I'm a patient man, Rachel. Take your time. I trust what the Lord gives me is good, and He surely brought you to me. I'll wait. The Howards live just over the rise. They raise sheep. I made a lot of cattlemen angry when I allowed Stephen to buy his flock of sheep. But a man with a family of women had little chance at raising cattle."

Thankful to be on another subject, Rachel smiled. "What are they like?"

"Since Stephen died, they are a family of women. Nina is the mother. Then there is Aileen, Bridgette, Cassidy, and Darby. All beautiful girls. Young women, actually. And all of them stubborn as sheep when it comes to that feud."

134

"Will Aileen be safe at the Murphys?"

"I think so. If I didn't, I wouldn't have made the arrangement. The Murphys are rough men, but honest. Mostly hard working. Apart, either family would be a credit to any community. But when they're together, they fight like rabid animals. Craziest thing I've ever come across. I thought the feud would die down as the kids got older, but if anything, it's gotten worse. This is their last chance. If the families don't get along, I'll have to kick them out of the valley and Shirleyville."

The team strained up a hill. Reaching the top, Rachel looked below and saw a neat yard and cabin below. She couldn't get Aileen out of her mind. The fear she must be facing at living in a strange house with men she didn't know. That part, Rachel understood very well.

Chapter 13

The judge gazed at the peaceful Howard home and felt regret at the turmoil he was inflicting on the family. Though they were as deserving as the Murphys, he hated the idea of putting any hardship on the women, but having Daniel around would be a help. Of that, the judge was thankful and sure.

Cassidy met them at the gate.

The grim frown on her face said all the judge needed to know. "Is Aileen ready?"

"Yes, sir. I hope you know that what you're doing is wrong. Dead wrong."

He nodded at her. "You just remember that your rowdiness played a part in my decision. If my men hadn't come upon you and Ronan, one of you might have been hurt or worse."

"It wouldn't have been me." She tossed her head, sending her blond mane flying in defiance.

The judge stared at her, wanting to say more but knowing it would be pointless. He chose to ignore the girl and instead, helped Rachel from the wagon. "We'll go on up to the porch. I thought you could comfort Nina."

"Yes, Sol. I'll help in any way I can."

Nina met them at the door. "Judge." Her eyes darted to Rachel. "Ma'am."

Rachel held out her hand. "I'm Rachel. I'm sorry for your loss."

With a nod, Nina turned to him. "Which loss would that be? My husband or my daughter? I hope you know I'm not agreeable to your decision, Judge. But you left me no choice. I want your guarantee that my daughter will be safe in that den of unholy men."

"You have my word, Nina. I'm leaving one of my men there for a few days to watch. Going to leave another one here just to make sure Daniel is treated right, and he respects you women. I don't expect any trouble out of any of you."

She frowned and crossed her arms but held her peace.

Aileen came outside, satchel in hand. "I'm ready, Judge." She said the words resolutely. Not whining. Not fearful.

He held out his hand and escorted her to the wagon. Then he helped Rachel. "Nina, you can visit each other on the weekends. In town. As long as there is no trouble that is. First sign of any and that's the end of the visit."

Nina glared at him. "Won't be any trouble from us. You watch those Murphys. They're the troublemakers."

The judge glanced at Cassidy. "Right. Let's go."

He climbed into the wagon and sat beside Rachel, thankful that she was with him. "Yates, you stay here a few days. Help out where you can and mind your manners."

The ranch hand nodded. "Yes, sir." But the grin on his face as he watched Bridgette walk up from the barn gave the judge pause. Still, his men knew better than to disobey. Yates would do right.

The judge slapped the reins and headed down the road. "It's not far to the Murphys. Maybe a couple hours ride by wagon."

No one said a word. The judge found the quiet a bit disconcerting. Women were seldom at a loss for words. And he had two in his wagon who hadn't said a thing. Both were apparently deep in their own thoughts. Probably best to leave it that way. He sure didn't want to listen to crying females for two hours.

As they pulled up to the Murphys, the judge was pleased to see that the place had been cleaned up, painted, and a good-sized new room added to the cabin. "Looks like your room is finished."

Aileen huffed. "My room is back at home. A slave doesn't have a room."

"You're not to be a slave to anyone. Just part of the family."

He stopped the wagon, but before he could get down, Aileen jumped out.

"As the only woman in this house, I'll be a slave all right."

The judge hopped down and caught her hand, taking the satchel from her. "I'll see to it that you're not. You'll help out, but you're not going to be their slave. In fact, I'll see that they do your bidding."

Her green eyes flashed, but she held her tongue.

The judge looked around and then saw Ben come from the house.

Ben walked up to him and took the satchel from his hand. "Aileen, welcome to our home. I heard some of the conversation. You'll not be a slave. Told my boys we're going to treat you like an honored guest. Show you and the judge that the Murphys are men of their word." He shrugged slightly. "For Anna's sake. She'd want you to be treated like a daughter. A princess. And that's what we're going to do. Right boys?"

Daniel was beside him. "Yes, sir."

Adam and Thomas came up from the barn. "Yes, Pa."

The judge helped Rachel from the wagon. "Ben, boys. This is my intended bride, Rachel Dowd."

Ben took off his hat. "Pleased to meet you, Ma'am." He turned to the judge. "Want to have a look at the girl's room? We did a good job of it."

The judge grinned. He'd already had the report from his men that they'd done most of the work. "Sure. We'll get Aileen settled in and then see Daniel back to the Howards."

Daniel stood next to Aileen. "I can get there myself, Judge. No need to take the time. All I own will fit on my horse."

"All right. I'll trust you."

Daniel escorted Aileen to her room. "We put an outside door. So, you don't have to go through the house to get outside if you don't want to. I think you'll like it."

She smiled at him. First smile the judge had seen her give all day.

Surprisingly, the house was clean, too. The Murphys must have done more cleaning this last week than they'd done in years. The new room was big and nice. Aileen fingered the dresser and the bed.

She glanced at him and then her eyes slid past to Daniel. "Thank you. It's nice."

Rachel hugged her. "If you need anything, send word, and we'll see to it."

Ben shook his head. "Murphys can take care of their own. We'll see to the girl. She doesn't even have to cook if she doesn't want to."

The judge almost laughed. After a week of men fixing the meals, Aileen would probably beg to cook for them. "As long as she's treated well, that's all I want. And I'll be checking."

Everyone left the room except Aileen and Daniel. The last one out, the judge turned just in time to see Daniel's hand slide from hers. Well, perhaps those two had their own plan to stop the feud.

He guided Rachel outside and to the wagon. "Daniel, I expect you to leave when we do."

The young man nodded, took his horse and led it toward the wagon. "I'll ride out with you."

141

The judge looked toward the cabin, but Aileen hadn't come outside. "Be good to her, Ben. I'm trusting, you."

"We'll be good to her. You just tell us when this arrangement is over."

"That's up to you and the Howards. When you two families can get along, that's when it will be over. Not until." He flicked the reins and swung the team out of the yard. The judge's heart groaned at what he'd decreed, but there'd been no other way.

He took his time getting home. He wanted the time with Rachel, but she seemed deep in thought and not interested in talking.

He stopped the horses at a creek and let them get their fill of water. "I've always loved this spot. Want to get down and walk a bit?"

Rachel's eyes lit up. "I'd love to."

He helped her down, and they walked along a path. He picked a daisy and held it out to her. "You said you like flowers. What kind?"

"Oh, we didn't have money for very many. We had one rose bush. A bright pink one that filled the air with a beautiful fragrance. Then I had a few Phlox and Primrose. Some wildflowers the children dug up and planted around the house. Mostly, I grew vegetables for the family meals."

She held the flower gently in her hand and fingered the petals. "Sol, I know very little about you. What do you like?"

Her question took him by surprise. What did he like? He rarely entertained such ideas. As a young man, he had dreams and hopes of amassing a fortune. Now, he'd done that. What was left?

Twirling the flower in her hand, she pointed it at him. "Well?"

"Horses. A fine spirited horse to ride across the plains. Sunsets. When the sun splashes the clouds with vibrant colors. I like justice. Settling disputes not with a gun but with the law. The Lord. He gets me through the hard times. Gives me hope. Brought you to me."

She stepped back. "I can see that I will have to learn to ride, then. And watch the sunset with you. You're aptly named Solomon. I've already seen you bring one wise decision to this wild land."

He waited. What was her view on God? He'd not thought to ask if she was a believer. He took it for granted that most were.

As if understanding his thoughts, she turned from him and rested on a boulder. "As for the Lord, I believe. But He let me down. Took Frank from me. My home. I'm not sure I can trust Him again."

He stood next to her. "Not even with me?"

She shrugged. "I'm not sure. I don't know you. I believe you're a good man. I just can't get over the fact that you could love me when I have nothing to give to you. There are countless women younger and prettier than I am. I have no money only ten children." She gazed into his eyes. "I'm just not sure I believe you could truly love me this quickly."

He smiled at her. "I want you to be honest with me. Always. I didn't plan on caring for you so quickly, but it happened. The moment I saw you, come around the stage." He paused to collect his thoughts and breath. "And like I said, I'm a patient man. You've already won my heart. I trust the Lord that I will win yours."

She blushed and sniffed at the flower still in her hands. "Perhaps." She rose. "I do need to get back to my children." She frowned slightly. "I'm afraid there are already ten others pulling at my heart."

He helped her to the wagon. "I won't push them out, but I believe your heart has room for me. I believe you'll want me. Soon."

In the wagon, she sat perhaps just a little bit closer to him than she had before. She smiled at the flower. "I did notice something between Daniel and Aileen. Have they been courting one another?"

"Doubt that seriously. Their parents wouldn't allow it. But since you mention it, I noticed Daniel holding her hand. Briefly, but I think there was also something in their eyes for one another. Thought it interesting myself."

She laughed. "I agree. Wouldn't that be something. Their marriage would surely end the feud."

"Or make them cast offs from both families."

"You don't think Nina or Ben would disown their own flesh and blood?" She stared at him with a wide-eyed innocence.

The judge grinned. "Before now, I think they'd have done just that. Now, with Daniel living in the Howard home and Aileen at the Murphys, that may just be the plan the Lord had all along."

She smiled. "You may be right."

He grinned to himself. She didn't say more, but perhaps there had been a breakthrough for Rachel and the Lord. Just maybe, she was beginning to see how good God was. Yes, he'd suffered loss, too. When Clara and Shirley passed on, he thought he'd never have another good day. Then ever so gently, the Lord wooed him back to life. Showed him a sunset that left him in awe. Ran a beautiful horse by him. Or just filled his heart with love by gently smoothing the craggy places that his daughter and wife's leaving had created. It had taken him years to see that the Lord hadn't taken his family for evil reasons.

They lived in fallen world. As a judge, he reckoned with that daily as fallen people paraded in front of his bench with the foul things they'd done to one another. It was a hard world they lived in. One that his wife and daughter had passed from. He took great comfort remembering that they were in paradise, and someday, he'd go to them.

Until then, he was to live here, now. Not in regret and wailing for the past, but in thankfulness for what he had, not what he'd lost. Yes, he surprised himself with the deep feelings he already had for Rachel and even her children. Yes, he'd have to win over William and a few of the other older ones. But like he told her. He was patient.

And sooner or later, he'd win her heart.

Chapter 14

A week had gone by, and the judge still didn't have Rachel's heart. He chided himself with all his talk that he was a patient man. Seems his patience came with a time limit. He did have seven of the children won over. The younger ones followed him when he was in the house. Penelope pestered him daily about getting a horse. Benjamin tried to remain aloof like his older brothers but wanted to learn more about the law and spent time in the study looking at the law books and asking questions about cases the judge had tried. The boy was smart and sure to make a good attorney.

The three oldest, William, Sarah, and James kept their distance. At times, the girl would look longingly at him as if she were battling within herself. The judge decided to give them time. He knew they must feel conflicted with loyalty to their father.

He could feel the same battle within himself. What would Clara and Shirley think? He thought he knew. They'd been very giving. Even Shirley, at only sixteen, wouldn't have wanted him to live alone.

Clara gave him a bit more of a struggle. At times, he was glad that Rachel had not agreed to marry last week. He wasn't ready either. There would have to come a day when each of them would have to let their loved ones go and join the living.

Already, his image of Clara was fading. He hoped Rachel would soon see him and not her husband. The judge glanced at her. She was sitting on the settee by the window, reading one of his books. Warmth filled his heart and took the edge off his disappointment. Still, he was going to have to ask the Lord for more patience. He hadn't thought it would take this long to win Rachel over.

Matt bolted into the house. "Boss!"

The judge entered the foyer. "What is it?"

"The oldest kid, William, rode off just after noon and his horse came back."

Rachel ran into the room. "William. Is he hurt?"

"I don't know Ma'am. The horse was all right. Might have got off and the horse ran home. They do that." Matt kept his gaze steady and voice even.

For that, the judge was appreciative. The fear on Rachel's face had come on fast. He went to her and put an arm around her. "It happens all the time. Even to seasoned hands. Horses get barn happy and have only home and food on their minds." He looked at Matt. "Did William say where he was going?"

"Nope. Never does. Hardly says a word to any of us." Matt stopped.

The judge read his foreman. William wasn't a favorite with him or the men. The boy kept to himself. When he was around them, he had a sour look and attitude to match. "Get some men, and we'll look for him."

Rachel hung onto his arm. "Please find him. I couldn't bear it if anything—"

"Shh. We'll find him. He didn't say anything to you, did he?"

She shook her head. "No." Then she looked up at him. "Last night, he did mention the Howards. That girl, Bridgette."

The judge hoped his face remained neutral. If that boy thought being with Bridgette was a good idea, he was in more trouble than his mother could imagine. He patted Rachel's hand. "We'll start that direction. Most of the men are at the ranch today, so we'll have plenty to go and look for him."

Worry clouded Rachel's usually sparkling eyes. "Please bring him home."

"Matt, get some men." The judge turned to her and shocked himself by wanting to kiss her as if they'd been married for years and he was just giving her a peck on the cheek to reassure her. Fortunately, he held back and didn't embarrass them both. "I'll bring him back."

Outside, clouds to the north gave him another reason to worry. He had no idea what William understood about life in the wilds of Montana. The judge figured it was little. "Matt, you spread the men out on the different trails. I'll head over toward the Howards. I don't like the look of the weather. I'm sure he didn't take a coat with him."

"No, but he did have water." Matt led the judge's horse from the barn. "Figured you'd want the black."

"Thanks. I'll go to the Howards."

"Want me to go with you?" Matt, always faithful, stared at him, worry creasing his brow.

"No, you direct the rest of the men. I'll be fine." What the judge didn't tell him was he felt it important to have a talk with William, alone away from Rachel and Matt. A competition of sorts was growing between the two young men, and the judge didn't like the idea. He didn't need another feud.

The judge mounted and rode the black toward the Howards, praying he could find the boy. Man really. "Lord, You brought Rachel and her children to me. Show me a way to William's heart. Help me find him. He doesn't trust me. I can see it in his eyes. And his mistrust is holding Rachel back."

The judge let the horse lope along the trail. Despite the clouds, the day was nice and still warm for October. If William had plans to seek out Bridgette, the judge would have to talk to Rachel about her son. Then again, William was twenty. Old enough to live his own life. Not like he would take fatherly advice anyway.

Bridgette wasn't a bad girl, but she was female through and through and knew it. She used her wiles to turn men into jelly. He'd seen it. Stephen had talked to him about his fears for his daughter. The judge decided he better pray for Daniel, too.

Then again, perhaps he didn't have to worry about Bridgette where Daniel was concerned. Not the way he and Aileen had looked at one another. Returning his focus to the problem at hand, the judge rode atop a ridge, rested his horse, and shouted. "William!" Only the call of birds bustling about in the afternoon sun answered.

He patted the black's neck. "I'm going to have to give you some kind of name, aren't I? Can't go on calling you the black. Where is that boy?"

He was almost to the Howard's road when the first cloud smothered the sun. A cool gust from the north signaled it meant business. A chill traced across his shoulders. The weather this time of year could turn fast and deadly. William should know better, being from Minnesota, but the boy was stubborn.

The judge paused, shook out his jacket, and yelled once more for William, but the wind had turned harsh and whipped his voice back to him. He wasn't far from the Howards. He just prayed William was there. He reined the stallion back to the road, angry that William had worried Rachel.

Almost to the Howards, the judge, head down to block the wind, saw William walking toward the Howard cabin. At least the boy had sense enough to know where to go. The judge rode up to him. "I've got the whole ranch out looking for you. You all right?"

William looked up at him without any joy at seeing him, only the same unruly disgust the judge had become accustomed to. With a shrug, William pointed to the Howards' cabin. "I thought I'd pay a visit. I got down and the stupid horse ran off is all."

"We'll sit out the storm at the Howards." He took his foot out of the stirrup and held a hand out to William.

The boy hesitated, then took it and swung up behind him. "Was getting tired of walking. Horse left me some miles back. I was hoping the Howards would loan me a horse."

Thunder rumbled in the distance. "This time of year, it's not wise to battle the storms. We'll sit this one out at the Howards. Next time, you need to tell someone where you're going."

"I don't see Matt asking permission. He's not much older than me."

"Matt knows the land. He's been a ranch hand most of his life. You worried your mother." The judge could feel the tension behind him as if a lit piece of dynamite rode with him.

William remained quiet.

Not able to let it go, the judge continued. "George and Matt will calm her down." He hoped they could. By the sound of the storm, it meant to assault the area with a vengeance. Rachel would worry. About William. Would she worry about him, too?

William huffed. "I wanted to see Bridgett. Met her in town last week and told her I'd come by. There weren't any clouds when I started out."

"This time of year the weather can change quickly, but you're free to do what you want, William. It's a good idea to let someone know where you're going. For cases like this." He stopped the horse in front of the cabin.

William slipped down and held the horse. "I'll take him to the barn."

"Thanks. I'll be inside."

The judge knocked on the door, and Daniel opened it. "Judge, come to check on me?" He grinned and opened the door.

"Sort of. William was on his way over here, and his horse took a notion to run home without him. There's a storm, so I thought we'd stay here until it's over."

Daniel eyed the darkening sky. "Storm is right. I better go round up Cassidy. She went to check the sheep. I spend more time getting her out of trouble than anything else. I don't know how she survived this long without a big brother." He grinned, grabbed his hat and coat, and ran out the door. He stopped William and the two talked and then headed toward the pasture together.

The judge went into the cabin and sat down near the fire. "I think it's going to be a cold night."

Nina came out and sat beside him. "Yes, my knee is telling me it could snow. When I was a girl, I got kicked by the old plow horse. To this day, it gives me trouble when snow is in the air."

"How are things working out?"

She sat back and sighed. "Good. Daniel has been a godsend for us. He's a strong young man and not afraid of work. Not at all what I thought he'd be like. Your plan seems to be working at least where Daniel and my family are concerned. The girls, most of them, love him like a brother. I was a little worried about Bridgett. You know how she can be. But she treats him like a brother, mostly."

"Glad to hear things are working out. If the weather clears for the weekend, you can go into town and check on Aileen. I expect to hear the same good news from the Murphys."

Loud clomps signaled the boys had found Cassidy. The door blew open, and the three of them ran inside.

Cassidy plopped in front of the fire. "Snowing. Bet your knee is sore isn't it Mama?"

"Yes dear, it is."

Bridgett came from the kitchen. "Dinner will be ready in a few minutes. We have turkey thanks to Daniel. He's a good hunter." She noticed William and smiled, and not at all a sisterly smile.

The judge chuckled to himself. William had better watch it or he'd be in trouble with that girl. The judge hoped the boy would be a little more sociable towards him after rescuing him, but by the angry looks William sent his way, no deal. He'd have to come up with some of his wisdom to make peace with the boy.

^^^

Rachel held in her tears to keep the children from seeing how worried she was. William was missing. She darted a look outside, and the falling snow gave her no comfort. He could freeze to death out there. What if William was badly hurt? She couldn't bear the thought of losing someone else.

To the children's delight, George brought a plate of cookies. He offered her one, but her stomach rebelled at the idea. There would be no comfort for her. Not until she saw William come through that door. Her mind

157

wouldn't rest until she admitted it. That wasn't all. Sol. She was worried about him, too. If she was to be honest with herself, she cared for him. More than just as a partner in a marriage of convenience.

George handed her a warm cup of tea. "Judge find boy. They be awright. You see. No worry." He grinned and returned to play with the children.

She gazed at her youngest devouring the cookies and thought how she should stop them so they didn't ruin their dinner. But none of that mattered at the moment. Had she made a mistake coming to this wild land? William said he hated it and didn't like Sol. He was against her marrying the judge.

Why, he wouldn't say. She couldn't get him to open up. Since Frank's death, her oldest had clammed up and refused to talk. He took over right away as the man of the house and got odd jobs to help out, but he remained aloof from talking over his feelings. His dreams. He'd planned to follow in his father's footsteps and farm, but when Frank died, it was as if Williams dreams had died with him.

She sat by the window and gazed at the swirling snowflakes. Any other time and she'd have thought how beautiful it was. Now, they symbolized death. They'd buried Frank in a snowstorm.

Sarah walked softly to her and sat on the arm of the big chair. "Mama, they'll be all right. I know it. The judge, he knows the land. He'll find William and stay somewhere warm for the night. Tomorrow, when they come in you can scold William for leaving and not telling anyone where he was going. And while you're at it, talk to him about his attitude. He's rude to the judge and Matt."

Rachel hugged her daughter. "I will do just that. I believe they'll come home safely, too. I'm just a little worried." That wasn't exactly the truth, but she didn't want Sarah to worry.

"Mama, I like the judge. He's good and kind. You are going to marry him, aren't you?"

Was she? She thought so. She laughed lightly. "We are getting married. We just wanted a little more time to get to know one another."

Sarah kissed her cheek. "Good. I love it here. I'd like to teach school. The judge said they don't have one here but need one. I sent a letter to a college to find out what I need to learn to become a teacher. From what the judge says, not much." She giggled. "He said as long as

I know more than the students, and can read, I can teach. He'd see to it that a school was built and we had all the books we needed." She glanced at her siblings. "Goodness knows, I have a schoolroom full just in this family."

Rachel laughed. "Yes, you do. In fact, that is an excellent idea. In all the turmoil of the move out west, I completely forgot about school lessons. I'll talk to Sol when he returns." Her heart skipped. If he returns. Oh God, please let him return with William.

Chapter 15

The judge looked out the window. "Snow is still coming down. All right if we stay here the night?"

Nina grinned. "More than all right. You're always welcome in my home, Judge. You too, William." She turned to face Daniel. "It's cold in that barn. Why don't all three of you men camp out here in front of the fireplace?"

Daniel grinned. "Thank you. I was thinking on how it would be a cold night tonight."

Sewing the last stitch to a button, Nina put the shirt down. "I think we need to make that room for you like they did for Aileen. I do hope she is warm tonight."

"Knowing my Pa and brothers, they'll make sure her wood box is full and the fire warm for her. They'll be good to her."

The judge grinned to himself. Seems his plan was working on the two feuding families. He'd yet to hear a cross word between Daniel and any of the Howards. Cassidy had a glare in her eyes a time or two, but she'd held her peace.

"I'm glad to see you're all getting along." The judge rubbed his arms and scooted closer to the fire.

"I'll have some of my men come over and help you winterize the cabin. Daniel, maybe you can take note of what's needed and let me know."

William stood. "I'll help. Not like I'm doing anything at the judge's home."

The judge almost remarked that he could fix that, but he held back. Now wasn't the time. Somehow, he and William needed to come to an understanding.

Nina went in the kitchen and returned with a steaming coffee pot. "Warm coffee anyone?"

She filled his cup. "When is that wedding going to take place, Judge?"

He took a sip and let the warm liquid chase away the chill. "Soon. I'll be sure you know about it. And of course, you and your daughters are all invited." He almost added as long as they didn't fight with the Murphys but thought better of it. He'd make sure they sat away from each other.

After another sip, he noted a bit of disappointment in Nina's eyes. He'd have to make sure not to be alone with the woman. Odd enough to stay in her home for the night. At least William was here to dispel any questions about his motive or goings on. He didn't think Rachel to be the jealous type, but then what would he think if she were to spend the night at the Murphys?

Nina, poured him another cup of coffee. Out of the corner of his eye, he caught William watching him. The judge would make sure not to be alone with Nina or overly friendly to her.

"Yes, we'll be married soon. I tell you, I can't wait." He paused. That didn't sound quite right, and the look on William's face told him he better say something else. "I've been alone far too long." He cringed. That didn't sound good either. And William's face was now red. "Rachel is a fine woman."

The judge wanted to go on, but William was taking everything he said wrong.

Then Bridgett walked into the room. Or he should say, sauntered in her most seductive manner. The girl was pure female, and her swaying ways didn't go unnoticed by William. If the boy's face had been red with anger earlier, it was beet red with embarrassment now. At least Bridgett had drawn William's focus away from him.

Bridgett sat on the floor between William and Daniel. "It is chilly in here. Think you boys could stoke the fire for me."

William nearly fell over getting to the poker and the fireplace. Daniel merely rolled his eyes and stood. "I'm going out to check the stock and bring in my bedroll."

Cassidy got up. "I'll look in on Skye. Guess the sheep will be all right."

Daniel grabbed his coat from the peg, and then took one to give to her. "Should be. They got that woolly coat on them. Besides, this storm is light. I figure the snow will be gone by noon tomorrow."

Bridgett glanced his way. "Why Daniel, I didn't know you knew so much about the weather. Whatever did we do without you?" She laughed and wrapped a blanket around her.

Daniel ignored her and waited for Cassidy to get her jacket on. He darted a look at the judge and shook his head before heading out the door.

William started to rise. "Maybe I should check on your horse, Judge."

Bridgett took hold of his arm. "They'll check on him. Why, Cassidy loves horses more than people." She grinned and looked slyly at the judge. "You stay here, William, and help me stay warm. Sometimes I wonder what we are doing in this freezing country. Where are you from?"

William grinned all over himself. "Minnesota. Just as cold there as here. We had a farm." He stopped for a moment as his eyes went to a place in the past. "I always wanted to be like my father. A farmer. Grow wheat and corn. Keep my hands in the rich black earth."

Bridgett frowned. "I want to live in the city. A big city like Chicago, or New York. Anywhere away from here and sheep. What possessed father to think we should raise the stinky animals is beyond me."

Nina slapped her hand on the chair. "That is enough, Bri. Your father was a good, hard-working man. He realized early on that raising cattle would be much too hard for a family of girls. Sheep we can handle. And they've done fine by us too. If you'd care to learn to use the wool, you could earn a decent wage. Darby and Aileen have both made extra money by making wool jackets."

The judge nodded. "I've got one of them. I tell you one thing, I thank those woolly critters of yours every time I put that jacket on."

Bridgett snuggled closer to William. "Just the same, my dream is in a big city. The man I'm going to

165

marry is going to take me there. Maybe he'll be a lawyer like you Judge."

The sultry way she stated that last sentence didn't go unnoticed. By him or William. To say she made him uncomfortable would be a near lie. The judge warmed his hands around the coffee cup. "Well, you can see where I live. Give me the wide-open prairie any day over the city. You might just find that cities aren't as exciting as you make them out to be."

Bridgett tossed her head, sending her red locks waving in William's face. The poor boy looked lost and in trouble. She pulled on William's arm. "Did you see Chicago on the way out here?"

He nodded. "It was crowded and brown. I didn't like it at all."

Darby, the youngest, and all of fifteen rose from her seat at the table and sat on the other side of William. "I love to work in Mama's garden. To see things grow."

William smiled at her. "I know what you mean. Plant a small seed in the rich earth and then watch as the seedling comes up all tender and bright green. Soon, you have the fruit of the earth. It's a wonder I hope I never tire of."

Bridgett rolled her eyes and scooted away from him. "Well, I am not going to be stuck in the country all my life."

The judge smiled to himself. Seems Darby had ideas about William herself. He sat back in the chair and enjoyed the warmth of the family. He thought of Rachel and hoped she wasn't worrying too much. He couldn't wait to see her again. And the children. He found himself missing them as well. Penelope and her horse questions. Annie and Kathleen and the twins. Sarah's nice welcoming smile. Julia who looked so much like her mother. Benjamin and James who were just shaping into who they might become.

This was going to be a long night.

^^^

Rachel put the children to bed, went to the kitchen and made a cup of tea, and sat by the window. Waiting and watching, her heart groaned to know that William was safe. None of the ranch hands had found him. Sol had not returned either.

He was handsome. Kind. Well-off. He was good to her children, and for the most part, they liked him. What was her problem? Her fear? Even as she asked, the answer pushed through her mind unbidden. The wedding night. The intimacy. The idea that another man would have his way with her, and the terrible truth was that she was attracted to him. And then there was the fear, that loomed like a ghost. She'd lost Frank, and a part of her heart had died with him. Was there enough of her heart left to give to Sol?

The snow stopped, and the moon shone brightly on the diamond-like white powder. She took another sip and smiled as she remembered another time. She was worried about their crops after an early snowstorm had buried them in a foot of snow. They couldn't afford to lose the corn.

Frank had sat her by the window and handed her a cup of tea. It was a night just like this one. Cold, brisk, and the snow had stopped. He took her hand. "Look at the diamonds, the Lord showered on our crop. You watch and see. The green shoots will not only survive but thrive. It's the Lords way of making them strong."

His words had comforted her, and he'd been right. That year, their crops flourished. Rachel sighed. "Oh, Frank. Why did you have to leave me?"

Could she really be Sol's wife if Frank's memory haunted her? She had yet to let go of him. The good times and bad. The nights. Frank so close to her they

168

became one. How does a woman let another man into her life and heart?

When Sol returned, she'd have to be honest with him. Give him the choice of waiting for her to want him, or he could send her away. She'd not promise him what she couldn't give. No, she'd not lie to him.

Right now, she did not love him. Could not bear the thought of a wedding night. Even with all his promises, she was not ready.

Chapter 16

The morning came bright and with the promise of warmth. Already, the snow dripped off the roof making a plunking sound on the porch. The judge stretched his aching bones. He was too old to be sleeping on the floor. He glanced at William and Daniel. They were already awake and putting up their bedrolls.

Daniel turned to him and grinned. "We let you sleep. Already had breakfast. The girls were quiet as church mice. I'll let William borrow my horse, and you can bring it to town tomorrow. That is if you plan to go into town."

The judge nodded. "Saturday, we'll be in town. Thanks, Daniel."

"Sure. I hardly need him here anyway. Those sheepdogs are the darnedest things. The girls just walk out there and point and the dogs round those woolly critters up. Wish cattle were that easy."

"Stephen was wise when he sold off his cattle and bought the sheep. Perfect for a family of women. I've got another pup for Cassidy to train, too. She can pick him up anytime."

Nina brought him a plate. "I'm sure Cassidy will be over to get him. That girl loves animals. Judge, we saved you breakfast. Sorry you had to sleep on the hard floor. At our age, that's not an easy arrangement."

The judge hated the idea of admitting he was getting older, but she was right, that floor had never felt so hard. "Our age? Not like we're ready to be thrown out to pasture."

Sadness tugged at the corners of her mouth. "Since Stephen died, I feel ancient. Like every muscle in my body is deep in sorrow and too tired to move. Does it ever get better, Judge?"

With effort, he rose and went to the table to sit across from her. Slowly, he nodded. "Yes, it gets easier. The ache never goes away. Little remembrances ambush me, but yes, it does get better. Life is still good, Nina. You have your girls."

She grimaced. "Sorry, Judge. I wasn't thinking. Of course, I do have my girls. I don't know what I'd do without them." Her eyes narrowed. "I am missing one of them."

"Just temporarily. As soon as you two families can get along without tearing up the town and each other, she can come home." He glanced at Daniel. "You do have a son, now."

Nina grinned. "For that, I do thank you. Daniel, you've been a godsend. I don't know what we'd have done without you. Even if you are a Murphy."

Daniel took his hat from the peg by the door. "My pleasure. I was getting tired of living with my smelly brothers. Have to admit, I got the better end of the deal."

Nina put a hand to her heart. "I pray that Aileen is all right. They wouldn't hurt her, would they?"

"No, ma'am. We Murphys might be a wild lot, but we respect women. Ma taught us that."

Sadness blanketed the room in silence. The judge looked at his eggs and dug in. So much loss. His thoughts drifted to Rachel. She'd lost her husband. What was she thinking?

Darby ran and brought William his jacket. "I saw you were missing a button. I sewed it on for you."

He smiled sheepishly. "Thanks. That was nice of you." He turned to the judge and his smile and goodwill disappeared. "I'll get the horses ready. Mother will be worried."

The judge held back stating if William had thought of her before he left out on his own, she wouldn't be worried. Struggling with his own anger, he put his fork down. "I agree. We'll leave as soon as you get them saddled."

Daniel opened the door. "I'll get your horse saddled for you, Judge. Take your time eating breakfast. Mrs. Howard makes great biscuits."

The judge sat back in his chair. "Daniel seems to be settled in with your family."

"Yes, we did need a man around the house. For that, I'm thankful for your ruling, but I worry about Aileen."

The judge took a napkin and wiped his lips. "I read Ben the decree that he better see that she's taken care of. You'll see her tomorrow in town. Just make sure you keep a handle on Cassidy. She's the one that is likely to cause trouble."

Taking up the dishes, Nina chuckled. "That is one thing you don't have to tell me. Between Cassidy's wild nature and Bridgett's female wiles, those two drive me to my knees in prayer. Might tell William to watch himself. Bridgett set her eyes on him. Although, him wanting to be a farmer is likely to ward her away from him. That girl wants the city life. I tell you, Judge, sometimes I wonder where she came from."

The door opened, and William entered. "Horses are ready." He turned to Nina. "Thank you for taking us in."

"Bye William." Darby smoothed her hair and smiled.

The judge smothered a laugh. "I'll see you in town, Nina."

"We'll be there. We will all behave. I want my daughter back."

With a nod, the judge put his jacket on and went outside into the bright warming sunshine. Daniel held the black and waited for him to mount before letting go of the bridle. "That horse is feeling his oats today. Watch him."

"Always. He's still got a touch of the wild in him."

William rode up on Daniels big bay.

Without a word to Rachel's son, the judge reined the black to the road but kept him at a trot. He didn't relish the horse running wild over the snow and icy road. William stayed behind him. Apparently, not wanting to talk either.

The judge feared they'd never get along and the boy would become a wedge between himself and Rachel. Maybe even preventing the wedding. Not ready to let the boy hold out and become an obstacle, the judge slowed the black until William rode alongside him.

"Seems a couple of those girls thought a lot of you."

A grunt was his answer.

"I know you want to farm, but this is cattle country. Around here, sodbusters are looked down upon."

"We are farmers. All of us. Mother included."

"Our land is dry. Grassland fit for cattle. If you plow it up, the land will blow away. We don't have the rain to hold the earth down and for the crops to grow. Besides, most of the land is open range. The cattlemen around here won't take kindly to anyone putting up fences."

William glared at him. "All the same, I'm a farmer. You'll not make a cattleman out of me."

"No, don't suppose I will." The judge reined in his anger. "It's nothing personal. Just what the land will allow."

"Farming is what I know. What I always wanted. What my father taught me." He nudged the bay and rode ahead.

The judge held the black in, refusing the horse's desire to run. William needed some time alone. To think on his future. But the judge wasn't about to let his land go to ruin to be used as farmland. Already, he'd angered most of the valley by letting the Howards run sheep.

He'd thought it would be so simple. So easy. Order a bride to come west. Take care of her children and promise to look after them all. Yet, it seemed that at every turn there was some trouble. He had enough rooms for each child to have one of their own. But the girls wanted to sleep together. William didn't like him or his way of life. Rachel wasn't ready to be married. Try as he might, he couldn't reach her. She'd gotten where she didn't even want to talk about their wedding. Or even what she would like to do. He'd asked her if she'd like to travel, and she'd yet to reply.

Rachel's life revolved around the children. Which it should, but would there never be a place for him? Did she only want him because of his provision? In her letters, she had agreed to the wifely duties, but now, he wasn't sure how close he could even get to her.

The judge looked across the valley. How is it he could tame a land and all that was on it, but one woman kept him at arm's length with no end in sight?

"Rachel, what do I need to do to convince you I'd never hurt you?"

^^^

Rachel had just fed the younger children when she heard James and Benjamin shout. She wasn't the only one that had heard and soon her army of children ran outside. Most without their coats on, shouting welcomes to William and Sol.

She laughed at the twin's shouts of "It's Mr. Judge and William." It didn't go unnoticed by her that they mentioned Sol first. He'd won the hearts of her five youngest. The rest varied in their like or dislike of the judge.

William didn't trust him at all and made it clear he wanted to go back to Minnesota. Sarah was content, but then she was always content. James and Benjamin blew with the wind on how they felt. While Julia lamented that her father was gone. The girl couldn't overcome her grief and lived in regret. She rarely smiled. Only Sol's puppies had brought a grin to her face.

Running outside, Rachel couldn't stop the smile on her own face. Her son was safe. Her eyes lit on William and stayed on him. She should go to Sol. After all, he was the one who'd found her son.

Yet, her fear kept her eyes on her William. Sol, she wasn't sure how she would react. She'd spent the night in torment. What if he were hurt or dead? What if she loved Sol? What would Frank or her children think? There didn't seem to be any peace.

Sol rode up to her and dismounted. Holding the reins, he eyed her. "Rachel, we had to spend the night at the Howards. I found William on the road, and they were closer than home. Hope you weren't worried."

She swallowed and gazed at him. Her heart skipped. She shut down the feelings and smiled weakly. "I'm afraid that I worried. Ever since Frank died, well, a mother's heart fears losing her loved ones."

Regret stabbed her. He'd grimaced. She'd not let on how she'd worried about him, and he clearly had wanted to know she cared. She couldn't tell him. Not now. Not until things were settled. Not until she had room in her heart for him.

William took the reins from him. "I'll put up the horses." His words had been low and without feeling. William and Sol had yet to make peace. She could hear the division in William's voice and see it in Sol's eyes.

The younger children swarmed around Sol. He grinned, and his eyes lit up. He gazed at her and the light dimmed. He'd looked and found her wanting. She'd disappointed him. Worse, she had little she could do to remedy her lack of affection toward him. Not now.

Sol grabbed up the twins, one in each arm. "We better get inside. It's cold."

The twins shouted. "Mr. George made cookies."

"Well, let's go get some. And some warm milk to dunk them in, too." Sol ran inside with her children trailing behind as if he were the pied piper.

Sarah hung back. "Mother?"

"Yes?"

"Why don't you like him?"

"Sol?"

She nodded.

"I do like him. He's a wonderful man."

Sarah breathed in deeply. "You don't show it. He noticed. You barely looked at him. He's a good man."

"I know that, dear." Anger rose inside her. How dare her daughter question her. Yet, Rachel knew the anger was at herself. Sarah was right. Why couldn't she show the judge that she cared? "Let's go inside with the others."

Disappointed, Sarah nodded and ran inside.

Rachel helped the children with their milk and cookies and then took a cup of tea and left the room.

Sol joined her. "Rachel, is there something I've done or said that has upset you?"

Pretending innocence, she looked up at him and shook her head. "No. I'm fine. I just need a little time to adjust. For the children to adjust."

"You sure?" He sat next to her, concern wrinkling his brow. "I suppose my feelings came fast. The first time I saw you. I didn't plan it that way. I thought we'd slowly get to know one another." He grinned.

She kept silent and his grin faded.

With a shrug, he sat back in the chair. "I said I'd be patient. And I will, but I'd like you to tell me what I can do. If there's anything that would make you happier let me know."

She stared at him. Nothing came to her mind. Nothing. Yet, he required an answer. She closed her eyes and said a quick prayer. Then looked at him. "I don't know Sol. Everything is happening so quickly. I just need some time."

He looked like he wanted to say something, but thought better and remained silent. Trouble lined his face.

"Sol, don't worry. I will come around. I will." Even she didn't like the disbelief in her voice.

"Tomorrow, we'll go into town. I have some things to do in the courthouse, and I need to check on the Murphys and Howards."

Glad to have another subject, Rachel quickly asked. "How were the Howards doing with the Murphy boy in their house?"

"Good."

Now it was her turn to be disappointed. Seems the judge didn't want to discuss the Howards. She waited for more, but Sol didn't add to the conversation.

"I better see about the children's clothes for tomorrow. I thought I might buy them another outfit."

Sol nodded. "Whatever they need, and you, too."

"Thank you." Her heart beat as if filled with lead. Why couldn't she let herself feel?

Chapter 17

The judge rode Big Sandy and let William drive the wagon with Rachel and the children. Rachel hadn't seemed a bit upset by his choice to not take the buggy, and that bothered him. Instead of growing closer, they were drifting further apart.

Penelope called out to him, her little girl voice pricking his heart, warning him that it was already too late if he ever thought about not caring for this family. He couldn't bear the thought of losing the children. "Mr. Judge, can I ride behind you?"

The girl loved horses. Despite having the awkward picture of Big Sandy loaded with kids, he held the palomino back until the wagon was alongside him. "William, stop the wagon. Seems I need to take on a passenger."

The judge chuckled as she scrambled over the twins and climbed on the wagon rail. Her thin arms reached out for him. He grabbed her and settled her behind him. "Hold on tight."

"Can we run?" Her slim arms reached around his sides, reminding him of rides with Shirley hanging on behind him. He hoped she wouldn't mind. Surely, those who passed on into Heaven's domain where there were no tears or sorrow wouldn't begrudge those living on earth the joy of loving one another. If only Rachel could break free.

"Hang on." He nudged Big Sandy into a lope and delighted in the girl's giggling laughter.

Soon enough, they rode into town. He stopped by the courthouse and helped Penelope down before dismounting. "Go with your mother. She has shopping to do, and I have business."

"Thank you, Mr. Judge." She hugged him and ran to the wagon that William had stopped in front of the mercantile.

About to enter his office, the judge paused and glanced at Rachel, who was just about to enter the store. "Rachel, meet me for lunch in an hour."

She nodded and scooted the children inside the store.

He'd finished most of his paperwork when someone knocked on his door. "Come in."

Daniel held the door and waited while Aileen entered ahead of him.

The judge's heart sank. Trouble. Why else would they be here? Anger rose inside him as his imagination took hold of the possibilities for trouble in a household of wild men and one shy girl.

Daniel ushered her into the office. "Judge, we'd like to get married."

The judge nearly fell out of his chair. "Married? Did something happen at the Murphys? Married to one another?"

They nodded.

"How, I don't—"

Daniel took his hat off and held it in his hands. "We've been sneaking away for a year to see one another. I love Aileen. We waited until we were both of age. She turned twenty-one last month."

Sitting back in his chair, the judge stroked his chin and wondered what this would do to the feud. Perhaps, the solution had been coming on its own. "When?"

"Now, if you can. We'll tell our families at lunch. We figured it would be better to not give Pa or Mrs. Howard a chance to stop us."

The judge tapped on his calendar. "How will you provide for a wife, Daniel?"

"I've saved up enough to buy a small section. I figure on raising cattle."

"And your families, what do you think they'll say?"

Daniel gazed at Aileen and took her hand. "Before you made us live with each other's families, I didn't think we had a chance staying around here. Now, we both think there's hope."

"All right. You tell your families today, and I'll marry you next week."

"Today, sir. We're asking as citizens. I know you've married others."

He tapped on the Bible he kept on his desk. "Considering the feud, you might be right to already be married when you tell your families."

"Thanks, Judge." Daniel let out a whoop and picked Aileen up.

She smiled and kissed him.

The judge could see the love between them. See it in their eyes and the gentle way they touched and the shy, knowing smile she gave Daniel. The judge rose. "Wait right here."

He opened the door. "Matt, Yates, mind coming in here for a minute?"

His two ranch hands entered and took off their hats.

"If you two will stand over here by my desk. I'm going to marry Daniel and Aileen, and you two will witness the certificate of marriage. We want it done all legal so no one can come against them."

The judge faced the bride and groom and held out the Bible. "Daniel and Aileen. I hold this book out to you because it is the foundation for a good marriage. Knowing the history of your two families, I think you two are going to need to rely on the Lord more than most." He handed it to Daniel.

"If both of you will put a hand on the Bible, I'll get on with it."

Aileen put her hand over Daniels. "We're ready. And we're not afraid, Judge."

"I can see that. Just remember you're saying your vows over the Lord's book. They are for now and forever as long as you both shall live."

Daniel glanced at his girl. "I love her more than life, Judge."

The judge grinned. He could see that. Why he never saw it before he couldn't say. "Daniel Murphy, do you promise to love, cherish, protect, and provide for Aileen?"

"Yes, sir. With everything that is in me, I will love her forever."

The judge turned to Aileen. "Do you, Aileen Howard, pledge before those here and God that you will love, respect, and honor Daniel?"

"Yes, with all my heart."

"As Judge of this territory, I pronounce you husband and wife. Go and enjoy your lives together. Always turn to the Lord for guidance and wisdom. Always turn to one another in trouble. Always love one another and not let an argument reign between you after the sun sets. You may kiss your bride, Daniel."

After a long and passionate kiss, Daniel came up for air and grinned. "Thanks, Judge. We won't disappoint you."

They rushed out of his office full of love with the added exuberance of youth and hope for the future.

The judge grinned and looked at his ranch hands. "If you two will just sign here, I'll take the two their certificate. They just might need proof when they tell their parents."

The two signed, and grinned like cats with feathers surrounding them. Matt put his hat on. "I think I'll go to the diner. Heard the bride and groom say they were headed there. This is one showdown I don't want to miss."

The two men practically ran out of his office.

Laughing, the judge glanced at his pocket watch. He needed to be there to put out any fireworks from those two families. Besides, it was almost time to meet Rachel.

He grimaced at the thought, longing for what he'd just witnessed between Daniel and Aileen, but fearing Rachel would never give it to him. If she disliked him so, he'd rather her tell him outright. Kill his hopes now rather than let him hold onto them for no reason.

But the thought of losing her and the children left him breathless. So quickly, they'd all entered in his heart. Why didn't Rachel want him?

He rose from his desk, feeling older than he should. He took his hat from the peg and thought of Daniel and Aileen standing before him. The two of them so full of hope. And here they came from feuding families. Love had found a way for them.

"Well, then it will for me, too." The judge looked up. "I don't think You brought her all the way out here for us to have a mediocre relationship. I'd appreciate it,

Lord, if you'd tell Rachel she needs to fall in love with me. Thank you, Lord."

The heavy burden he'd felt in his heart lifted. He only needed to love her and her children. Even William. He'd come around. She would, too. He knew it. Believed it. There had been a reason that her letter was the only one he'd responded to. Something clicked in his heart that very first day. Soon, Rachel would admit she loved him.

He found Rachel at a table in the corner. She sat alone while her children sat at two tables pushed together near the back. He also noticed the Murphys and Howards sat across the room from one another. Aileen and Daniel sat at a table in the center. By the peaceful atmosphere in the room, the judge gathered they'd not shared their news, yet.

The judge stopped in front of his bride-to-be. "Rachel. You look lovely this morning. Not sure I didn't already tell you that, but your beauty deserves that I tell you again."

She glanced at him. "Thank you." She opened her napkin and set it in her lap. "You barely said a word to me all morning."

He nodded. "I'm sorry. Guess I was preoccupied with my own thoughts."

Rachel stared into his eyes. "Thank you for being patient with me."

"Even a saint has a limit."

Shock widened her eyes. Her gaze darted to the back of the room before returning to him. "I have so much to think about."

"Rachel, we both have a lifetime without one another. Not to forget, but to set aside. But there is coming a time when we need to pick up our life together. Get married. Be husband and wife. Forge a family out of our broken lives." He sat back in his chair, his appetite waning. "I've already accepted your children into my life. I want you, but until you decide you want to marry me—"

"It's not easy, Sol. There's Frank to consider, the children. William."

"Frank is as dead as Clara. Most of your children like me. William, is he the problem? I've tried. But he's as stubborn as you."

She gasped. "How crude for you to talk about our loved—"

"Your husband is dead. My wife is dead. We are alive. This is our time. I believe the Lord put us together. I'll admit, initially, I was lonely and merely wanted companionship. Someone to watch sunsets with and drink coffee in the mornings. Someone to tell about my day."

"I want that, too." Rachel's eyes moistened. "I've been lonely. Needing a man to—"

"To provide for you? Is that all? Because I need more than a business arrangement. I need to love someone and to be loved back by them. I told you I'd be patient, but my patience is dwindling. I will need to know by the end of this week if there is hope for us or not."

Tears spilled down her cheeks. "I'm sorry. I'll let you know."

A chair hit the ground and Ben's angry voice cut through the silence. "What! You married her! Are you crazy?"

The judge grimaced.

Rachel dabbed her eyes with the napkin and stared at him. "Did you know?"

"Not until they came to my office this morning. I married them less than an hour ago."

Soon, Nina's voice entered the fracas. "I like Daniel, but he is a Murphy. Your father would not have agreed to the marriage, and neither do I."

Aileen held onto Daniel. "We are married. Life is for the living not the dead. Papa wanted me to be happy. I know that. Yes, he and Mr. Murphy were engaged in a feud that damaged us all. But I don't believe either my Papa or Mrs. Murphy would want us to suffer any longer. The Bible says that God is Love. He would approve of our marriage."

Shouts from the Murphy men and the Howard women erupted, drowning out reason and thought.

The judge stood and was about to shout for them to get quiet or get out when Rachel came to his side. She put her hand on his arm. "God is love. Life for the living. Food for thought, I think." She looked into his eyes.

Sol took her hand. "From the first moment I saw you, I knew we had more than an arrangement together. I love you, Rachel."

Scuffling chairs broke their tender moment.

Sol patted her hand. "There are some things I must tend to." He let her go, but she grasped his hand.

"Sol, we are in this together. Perhaps I can help."

He nodded. "Maybe so, it's been a long time since I've had a helpmate. Shall we go?"

Together they walked between the angry families. Sol raised his hand and a tenuous silence settled over the diner.

"Daniel and Aileen came to me this morning to ask if I'd marry them. They're of legal age, and I agreed to. There is nothing you two families can do." He held up the certificate and handed it to Daniel. "They are legally married. Next week, I'll expect Adam to go to the Howards and Bridgette to go to the Murphys to extend the decree I issued and keep the peace."

Ronan blurted out. "Aileen said Bridgett can't cook. What good is she going to be at our house?"

Sol pointed his finger at the boy. "Your job is to take care of her. Understand?"

He nodded but grumbled.

Rachel took Aileen's hand. "I'm happy for you. I hope you'll come to our wedding. Tomorrow." She looked at Sol.

He smiled at her. "You're sure?"

Rachel's eyes opened wide. "Is there someone who can marry us?"

The judge laughed. "George. He used to be a minister. Methodist. He can marry us."

Sol ushered the two lovers toward the door. "Ben, Nina, the wedding is tomorrow if you want to come, but if you do, you best behave. That goes for all of you. I won't put up with any feud business on my land."

Outside, the judge caught Rachel's arm and pulled her to the side. "Rachel, I want you to be happy, not look at our wedding as a duty you must perform."

She wiped tears from her eyes. "No, no it's time. I need to for the children."

"Rachel, for us. For you."

"Yes, yes of course. For us, too."

Sol stared at her, saw the lie in her eyes. What did she have against him? "Is there someone else?"

With a gasp, she backed against the diner wall. "No. Of course not."

Riders galloped down the street, a wagon following.

He turned from her. "What now?"

Barrows jumped off his horse. "Judge, we were out with the cattle in the south pasture, and that gang shot up the Prouty ranch, killed Mr. Prouty before we could get there." He pointed inside the wagon. "You might not want to look, Mrs. Dowd."

The judge took Rachel by the shoulders. "Keep the kids inside."

^^^

Rachel shuddered at the thought of someone violently killed. After telling her children to remain seated, she stood by the door, watching Sol.

William walked past her and stopped. "I'm a man, Mother. I have to take my place in this land if we're going to stay." His eyes were stormy and warned her to not confront him.

"Be careful, William."

He glared at her. "I heard. You're marrying the judge. You don't need me."

"Oh, William. I'm sorry you feel that way. But I came out here to marry Sol."

He looked away.

"It's what I have to do."

He turned and faced her. "You don't even love him. How can you?"

She took him by the arm. "Listen to me. Sol is a good man. I do have feelings for him. I am sure in time we will have a good marriage."

"Well, it looks like you're being bought and paid for to me."

She slapped him and immediately regretted it. "I'm sorry, William. But you are wrong. I had no idea that Sol had money or a big house. And since we have been here, he has treated us all with respect and kindness."

Rubbing his cheek, William glared. "Father—"

"Father is dead. I am alive and need to go on living. And I choose to do that with Sol. I was wrong to put off my feelings to please you. All the other children are fine with our marriage. If you don't approve, you can go back to Minnesota."

He looked at her, hurt in his once defiant eyes. "If you want me to leave, I will."

Sol walked up behind him. "Neither I, nor your mother, want you to leave, but we won't stand in your way." He put an arm around her. "I hope you'll stay for the wedding."

William shrugged. "Not like I have anywhere to go."

Rachel shook her head. "William, I am most disappointed—"

Sol shook his head. "William, the man out there in that wagon, Dennis Prouty, he died alone. Oh, there

196

were some hands around when the outlaws came. But what I'm trying to tell you is that there was no one for him to leave his land to. It's all fine to amass great holdings, the biggest ranch in the valley, and enough gold to tide you over for ten lifetimes, but it's all meaningless if you have no one to love and leave it to. That's part of the reason I was glad your mother had children. A legacy for me.

"I had no idea there were ten of you. But it delights me. I only want to make your mother happy and provide for the ten of you. All ten of you. Including you. It wasn't until your mother and you children came to live with me that I felt rich again. A man works hard to provide for his family. To pass it on to those he loves. I hope you can understand that."

William stared at her and then Sol, but remained silent.

Rachel reached out to her son. "Tomorrow, you'll come to our wedding?"

He shrugged, and then turned to the judge. "The men going after the outlaws?"

"No, not this time. We're sure they're back in their hideout in the badlands. Too many canyons and places for ambush. I got a wire back from the man I asked to come as sheriff. He thinks he can get here next summer. Winter is coming and the gang will more than likely head south."

William nodded and went out to stand around the wagon with the Murphy boys.

Rachel sighed. "I don't know whether to be relieved or worried that he is with the Murphys."

Sol chuckled. "They're not bad. I think maybe William and I came to something of an understanding."

Rachel straightened his collar. "I would say so. I'm sorry it has taken me so long. You are truly a most wonderful man. I don't know what I was thinking."

He twisted his finger around a curl of her hair. "You were being a mother first. I'd expect that out of the kind of woman I'd like to marry. A kind, gentle woman. One so beautiful that she'd capture my heart at first sight."

She looked into his eyes and felt her heart warm. Perhaps, she already loved this man. By the tingles inside her, she was well on her way.

Chapter 18

The judge's neck itched where the fancy shirt rubbed him, but he wanted Rachel to be proud of him. He'd seen the change in her eyes. When she realized he only wanted to love her and her children.

And he did. God help him he had lost his heart and head to Rachel and her children. Even William held a place in his heart. The judge combed an unruly patch of hair and grinned. His heart had been empty for so long, it was ready to be filled.

William would come around.

A knock on his door startled him. He glanced at his pocket watch. He still had fifteen minutes. "Come in."

Sarah entered. "I wanted to, well, I needed to have a talk with you."

The judge nodded and went on tying his tie. "I'm listening."

"It's about Mother. I know you asked her if she wanted to travel."

That got his attention. He turned and faced the young woman. "Yes. I did."

She smiled. "Mother does. She always talked about Paris and London. If you can, and want to, take her there for your honeymoon. I talked it over with Matt and George, we can watch the place."

"You wouldn't mind?"

Stepping forward she hugged him. "I want mother to be happy. I believe you're the man who can."

"And William?"

"Don't worry, Judge. He'll come around. He's just stubborn."

The judge shoved an arm in his jacket. "So am I." His jacket on, he walked to the door. "Thank you for telling me about your mother, Sarah. I only want to make her happy."

"I can see that. Don't worry about us, I can handle the children."

Sol walked down the stairs and to the parlor. George had kept the children busy all morning decorating.

George beckoned him, wearing a purple robe instead of his Chinese silks. "This way, Judge. You stand right here." Grinning widely, the Chinaman nodded. "You might want to see your bride."

Sol turned, and his heart leapt as Rachel, escorted by William, walked toward him. Her eyes were bright and happy.

They reached his side and William put her arm in Sol's. He and the children retreated behind them and stood with the ranch hands of Rockin' C ranch.

George held a Bible out to him, just as he'd done with Daniel and Aileen. "Take this Word and hold it."

"Missy Rachel, you put your hand over his." George looked heavenward. "God, the Lord of all, we come to you this day to marry Judge Solomon Taggart and Rachel Dowd. Thank you that You, Lord, are love and have filled these two with Your Love to share with one another.

"Solomon, do you take this woman to love with all that is in you. To hold her in good times and bad. To protect her and provide for her."

"I do."

"Rachel, do you take this man as your husband. To love him. Respect and honor him in all your ways."

"I do."

"As a servant of God, I announce and proclaim that Solomon and Rachel are now husband and wife. Let no man come between you. Judge, you may now kiss your bride."

^^^

Rachel didn't wait for Solomon. She stood on her toes and put her arms around her husband. They met midway, and their kiss came together full of more love than she thought possible. She surprised herself with the love she felt for Sol. Complete and warm and full.

She met his gaze. "I love you, Sol. I'm not afraid anymore."

"Good, because I have a surprise for you. A wedding gift."

"Oh, I didn't—"

"You and the children are gift enough for me. I think we need a honeymoon to get to know one another. Say, maybe two months."

"I'm not—"

He kissed her lips quickly. "Shh, you've not heard it all. Abroad. England and France. Though they may not be the nicest in the winter, we can return again another time in the summer."

"Sol," she looked at her children. "Do you think we could?"

Sarah grinned. "Children."

As one, the children shouted. "We want you to go."

George nodded. "We take care of all. Me, Matt and William and Sarah. We be fine. Go and enjoy one another."

Rachel closed her eyes and nodded. "Yes, yes." She opened them and gazed at her man, Solomon Taggart. And the love she saw in his eyes mirrored the love she felt in her own heart.

She gazed heavenward and smiled. Yes, she could feel Frank's joy for her. She was alive and meant to live each moment of her life.

She caressed Sol's face. "I can't wait to go."

He took her in her arms. "Good thing you can't. I have the stage waiting for us."

"I have to pack."

"No, I don't think you do. I took the liberty of putting some things in a trunk for you. The rest we'll buy as we go."

Matt ran to them. "Buggy is ready."

Rachel sought William. He was standing alone, in the back of the room. She'd so wished he would come around, but as Sol had said, he was a grown man and would have to come to his own conclusion.

Turning her attention to Sol, she squeezed his hand. "I love you."

He kissed her lightly. "I loved you from the first."

"I was slow, but I'll make it up to you." She kissed him with all the tenderness and love in her.

^^^

Sol stretched and glanced at his sleeping bride. They'd been gone a week now. So far they'd only made it as far as Chicago. He wanted her to see the big city. Shower her with all the good things life had to offer. They'd eaten at the best restaurants. Seen plays. Bought her clothes fit for a queen.

He kissed her gently. "Rachel. It's morning."

She snuggled close to him. "Sol, we're not on the ranch. I don't think the city wakes up before eight." She sat up and studied him. "Is there something wrong?"

"No, nothing could be." He loved her so and relished the idea of loving her more each day. "Rachel, I was wondering. When you don't think I'm watching, I've seen tears in your eyes. I thought this was the right thing to do, but now, I'm not sure."

Her face paled. "Sol, what are you talking about? I love you. I was slow to come around, but now, I know we were meant for one another. I love you."

He caressed her face. "I was thinking that maybe you were missing the children. That maybe we should postpone our European trip until the summer."

Joy shone in her eyes. "Oh, Sol. Could we?"

"We can. I've already arranged for travel back—"

"Home." She kissed him. "Our home and our family. Oh, Sol. You've made me the happiest woman."

He hugged her. "I miss them, too. Got to thinking about Penelope and which horse she'd like to have. You know she changes her mind from a palomino to a sorrel, and then just the other week she wanted a black one like mine. Did I tell you, she named the black, Thunder. Said it wasn't proper to have a horse with no name."

"You have won over my children."

"Except for William."

"He'll come around. I did. And he did walk me down the aisle. I think that was a peace offering on his part."

Sol nodded. "I can take it as one." He kissed her again. "We better get ready. The train won't wait for us."

^^^

Sol helped her out of the buggy. "I can't wait to surprise them."

Rachel hugged him. "Me either. What a wonderful gift you've given me."

"I love you, Rachel." He looked at the big house with the windows lit yellow by the lamps. His house had never looked so much like home. He opened the door, and held it for her.

It was dinnertime and the children were gathered around the dining table. They bowed their heads and said the meal prayer with George. After the chorus of amens, Penelope let out a huge sigh. "I want Mama and the judge."

Larry pointed at them. "Mama, the judge."

Rachel beamed and ran but stopped and turned. "Sol, our children are anxious to see us." She held her hand out to him.

Taking her hand, Sol walked with her to the kitchen. "We thought we'd postpone the honeymoon until summer. Truth is, we missed you all too much."

The children ran from their seats and surrounded them. Rachel knelt and kissed each one. Her heart sang with joy when she saw that Sol had picked up the twins.

William got up from his chair and walked toward them. "I'm glad you're back." He shrugged, and gave a weak grin. "Both of you."

Sol set the twins down and shook William's hand. "It's good to be home."

Rachel hugged him. "It is good to be home."

^^^

Soft pounding yanked Judge Solomon Taggart from his dream. He threw off the blanket, and was about to swing his feet to the floor when he remembered the reason for his dream. He turned and stared at Rachel. Lately, the only dreams he had were about her. Good dreams and they seemed to spill out into the days. He kissed her gently. "The children are up."

Rachel opened her eyes and smiled. "Let them in, my love."

Sol wrapped his robe around him and handed Rachel hers. "All right children, come on in." He unlocked the door and stood back as the five youngest ran in and jumped in his oversized bed.

Penelope grinned at him. "Papa Judge, I decided I want a black horse like yours. I can name him

Lightning to go with your Thunder. And then we can ride over the plains at a gallop."

His heart full, Sol scooped her up and nodded. "Lightning it is. I'll have Matt start looking for just the right horse today."

Dressed in work clothes, William stopped outside the room. "If it's all right with you, I'm going to ride over to the Howards today."

Rachel started to speak and then looked to Sol. "What do you think?"

Sol smiled. "I think William is a man. It's his decision." He hugged her and then looked back at William. "If you want, ride Thunder for me. He needs a good work out."

William grinned and ran down the stairs.

Sol pulled Larry off a squealing Annie. "All right, I smell flapjacks. Let's get this day going." With a heart and home full of joy, he walked with Rachel as they went to breakfast with their family. Yes, she had been the one for him.

He let her go in front of him as he looked heavenward and smiled.

~~~~~~~~~~

Author's note:

I hope you enjoyed this story. Sol and Rachel will have their hands full with all those children, but I have fun thinking about their adventures. And of course, the feud is still on. Not sure how the two families are going to deal with Aileen and Daniel's marriage. Or if the Murphys will starve when Bridgette starts cooking for them.

Anyway, **Zebulon's Bride**, Book 2 is a bit of a diversion as Zebulon Benton and Amy make their way to Solomon's Valley. Along with a few other characters to add to Shirleyville. One of them being the sheriff who will get his own story in Book 3, The Sheriff's Bride.

Thanks for taking the time to read the story. Hope you enjoyed it and are looking forward to Zeb's story and the sheriff's.

*****If you enjoyed this story, please consider leaving a review. *****

5 stars = I loved it   4 stars = I liked it.   3 stars = it was ok.

Blessings,

Patricia PacJac Carroll

For more information, please contact

email ………….. **patricia@pacjaccarroll.com**

Web site………... pacjaccarroll.com

FB

https://www.facebook.com/PatriciaPacJacCarrollAutho r?ref=hl

Twitter   https://twitter.com/PacJac

Amazon page: Books by Patricia PacJac Carroll

If you'd like to be notified about new releases >**Sign up for my Newsletter

Author Patricia PacJac Carroll Newsletter____> http://eepurl.com/bpPmbP

Zebulon's Bride   Zeb wants freedom. His mother wants him married. Amy wants adventure.

Zebulon's Bride

Chapter 1

1882 April

Denver, Colorado

Zebulon Benton tore off his work apron, traded it for his jacket, and nodded at the young man walking inside the store. It was about time Jeremy came to watch the counter at Benton's Mercantile. Determined to leave the store, Zeb pointed at the first shelf. "The cans need straightening. I'm going out for a while."

With his usual happy smile, Jeremy sauntered over to the aisle and began moving the beans.

Satisfied that the store was covered, Zeb grabbed his hat and practically ran out of the store. Too bad it was only temporary. He walked down the street to the outskirts of Denver and tried to convince himself he would have to go back. An eagle screeched high overhead, soaring high and flying north. Free to go where he pleased.

Zeb kicked a rock down the road and tried to stop the calling in his heart to go to Montana. He'd been ten when an old mountain man sat on the bench in front of the store and told him tales of mountains that reached to the heavens. Of a sky so big, blue, and wide that you'd think it was going to come down and swallow you. Of a place where grass grew higher than a buffalo and gold nuggets lined the ground just waiting for a feller to come and pick them up.

"Just a tale." Zeb shrugged. Not like he could get away. Pa needed him to help with the orders and heavy lifting. And Ma, well, she always carried on how she couldn't bear to have another of her children leave home.

His sister, Monica, had up and married a Texas Ranger and moved to Texas. Zeb was happy for her. Texas might not have the mountains, but it was big and wild. He liked her husband, Gabriel. She couldn't have chosen a better man.

Pleasance had married the man she loved and moved to a ranch not too far from Denver by train, but she wasn't home.

"Zebulon Benton. Want some company?" By the way the female voice stretched out his full name as if she longed to own him, he knew who it was without looking back.

He didn't answer or veer from his course and kept walking.

She ran to him and matched his steps.

Unable to ignore her, Zeb glared at her. "Martha Lu, what are you doing out here? It's not safe this far from town." Her mother probably sent her out to snag him when he walked past their house. That or his own mother told her to find him. At twenty-six, he should be married, at least that's what his mother frequently told him.

The young woman frowned. "Now, that doesn't sound like you're happy to see me."

Well, he wasn't. Why did every woman in town think he needed to be married off? "I was going out to think. Alone."

She wrapped her arms around his. "It's a fine day for a walk. Mind if I join you?"

He drew in a breath of spring air and nearly coughed as the strong odor of verbena coated his lungs. She must have taken a bath in the stuff. "I was going for a walk to think. By myself." Apparently, she hadn't heard him the first time. He walked faster.

Martha Lu kept up with him. "You going to the meadow?"

"No." Of course, he *was* going to the meadow but not now.

"The creek?"

Zeb didn't answer.

"I have always liked you. We're of marrying age, and it's time for us to settle down and start a family."

He stopped so abruptly that she walked two steps past him.

Whirling around to face him, she pouted. "Zeb, we've known each other since we were children. I've always considered you my friend, even more."

Staring into her brown eyes, he disentangled his arm from hers. "I'll do my own choosing of where I'm going, and who I'll marry if I even choose to be married. Now, if you don't mind, I'm going to go and think. Alone."

Tears welled in her eyes, yet she kept her head high. "You're just as stubborn as an ornery mule. I only came out to be friendly. You go on by yourself then. And while you're at it, think how cold and lonely the nights will be." Face red, she ran back to town.

Zeb watched to make sure she made it to the boardwalk thinking on how well he understood the cold, lonely nights part. He'd considered seeking a wife. Trouble was, he really couldn't see himself growing old with Martha Lu or any of the other girls in town. Not that there was anything wrong with Martha Lu. She was handsome, pretty actually with her dark curls and red lips, but he didn't want to be tied down.

After he was sure that Martha Lu made it safely back, he turned and headed for Gambler's Creek. The bright, spring sun warmed him and soon, he shrugged out of his jacket and slung it over his shoulder. He had decisions to make. He picked his way up a rocky trail and then down until he came to the fast-moving creek.

Rapids sent white water over the rocks and crashing into boulders. The sound helped soothe the ache in his soul. How much longer he could remain at the store, he wasn't sure. Every day, he struggled to open the door and get ready for the customers.

He rested against a fallen log and threw stones into the water. Something was going to have to change. Either him or his circumstances. Pa ought to understand. He was the one who left his family in Missouri and came west to Colorado.

An eagle's piercing cry split the quiet. Zeb looked up through the aspen, searched for the bird and finally spotted it perched on the dead branch of a broken pine. "I hear you. We were born for the wild." Sorrow at his predicament led him to add, "Not for a life indoors."

Lowering his head, Zeb prayed. "God, I know Your Word says to honor your mother and father. I'm trying. I don't know how much longer I can stay and work in that store. It's not in my heart to do so. Either change me or set me free. Amen."

He waited but heard nothing more than the screech of the eagle and the rushing water. Both going somewhere, whereas he was headed back to town. With a sigh, he cut short the protest in his soul to leave and resigned himself to another day in the family store.

Made in the USA
Lexington, KY
19 December 2019

58875178R00134